Oliver Lambert has taken his photography skills and run with them. By the time he's thirty, he's made a name for himself and now has jobs whenever he needs them. He likes to be behind the camera, watching the world through a safe lens, protected from *actually* engaging with it.

An unexpected referral takes him somewhere he never expected—a kinky fetish ranch in the Muskokas, where men pay to play pony and trainers teach them how to behave.

Adam Marsland needs a visual record of the Braided Crop Ranch and it's been a while since the website photographs were updated. When he's given Oliver's name, he immediately hires the man to come for the summer session to immerse himself in the ranch and its activities.

Oliver is out of his depth, but the challenge of photographing the beautiful men at the BCR is something he can focus on. Safe behind the lens of his camera, Oliver finds the ranch to be seductive and shocking. He can't help admitting a fascination for the people who make the Braided Crop Ranch what it is.

But just because he knows how to take a great photo doesn't mean he's prepared for everything he encounters, especially when it comes to a recalcitrant ponyboy named Puck.

Contains: voyeurism, second-hand embarrassment, awkward conversations, a very introverted photographer, and several surprising developments, along with all the regular kink and pony play elements.

*Note: The timeline of *Hotblood* is prior to the events in *Stable Hand* but should be read either as the fourth book in the series or as a standalone.

HOT BLOOD

The Braided Crop Ranch, Book Four

AE Lister

A NineStar Press Publication

www.ninestarpress.com

Hot Blood

© 2023 AE Lister
Cover Art © 2023 Natasha Snow

First Edition, February 2023

ISBN: 978-1-64890-615-2

Also available in eBook, ISBN: 978-1-64890-614-5

CONTENT WARNING:
This book contains sexually explicit content, which may only be suitable for mature readers. Depictions of Smoking, discussion of auto accident/collision.

To my awesome readers and the members of Lister's Loop on Facebook.

CHAPTER ONE

AN UNEXPECTED INVITATION

OR

HOW TO RISE TO AN IRRESISTIBLE CHALLENGE

EDITING DIGITAL PHOTOS to make fruits and vegetables appear perfectly ripe, juicy, and seductive was not where I thought my life would end up.

When I'd chosen photography as the focus of my fine arts degree at the University of Waterloo in Southern Ontario, I had imagined somewhat more exciting subject matter. But most of my assignments these days involved long hours spent hunched on my elbows in the dirt, taking alluring shots of farm produce.

On my very fancy and expensive computer monitor, a ray of morning sunlight bounced off the red skin of a plump tomato. I'd tried several filters and a range of exposures to get it just right, but something wasn't working.

I clicked on another set of tools and looked for a different approach. While I perused the list, my phone pinged from where it lay on the desk.

I glanced at the screen to see a text from an unknown number:

> *Mr. Lambert, is it OK if I give you a call in a few moments? My name is Adam Marsland. I was given your name and contact info by Jaden Stevenson. I'm looking for a photographer.*

Since referrals had gotten me to where I was in my life at the moment—a recognized purveyor of outstanding photographic interpretations of reality—I texted Mr. Marsland back immediately.

> *Of course. Give me five minutes.*

I input Adam Marsland as a contact and stood from my chair. My neck cracked when I stretched it to the side, and again when I repeated the motion in the other direction. I was only thirty years old, but sitting in one position for too long was bad for anyone. I reached my arms up and over my head, feeling the pull in my muscles.

Moving into the kitchen of my small condo on Toronto's East Side, I grabbed a tumbler, pressed the button on my fridge for cold water, and watched the stream of liquid splash into the glass. It would be fortuitous if Mr. Marsland could offer me a contract for some images. I was booked up until mid-June but, after that, things looked a bit sparse.

I carried my drink to the living room window and gazed out on the city. Living on the fifteenth floor afforded me the luxury of a stunning view, even if the square footage was small. At least the finishes and upgrades in this unit were of the highest quality and done according to the latest trends. I'd been able to furnish the tiny apartment with quality pieces, like the Eames chair and a tan leather love seat from West Elm, since I didn't need many.

When my ringtone sounded, I walked back to my desk, put the glass down, and pressed the answer button, remaining on my feet since I'd been sitting for the past hour and a half.

"Mr. Marsland," I said.

"Mr. Lambert. Good afternoon. How are you today?"

"Fine, thanks. What can I do for you?" I asked, taking a sip from my glass.

Mr. Marsland cleared his throat, and I heard the click of a pen. "I'm hoping you can come to my ranch and take some photos for me. You come highly recommended."

I smiled, because it was always nice to hear that. "Thanks. Jaden mentioned me?"

"Yes. He thinks you'd be perfect for what we need."

"I'm pretty booked up at the moment. What time frame are we looking at?"

"I'd need you to spend part of the summer here, if you're available, and interested. You'll be compensated well and we can put you in a room at the main house during your stay."

Perfect.

"I do have most of the summer free at the moment. Are you talking three weeks? Six?"

Papers rustled on Mr. Marsland's end. "Six weeks. From mid-July to the end of August."

I walked back to my computer and put the glass down beside it. "And I'd be photographing horses? Riders? The landscape, too, I suppose?"

There was a pause, and he laughed. "We're not that kind of ranch, Mr. Lambert."

I narrowed my eyes at the red tomato that had tortured me with its saucy round form all morning. Mr. Marsland's comment intrigued me.

"Call me Oliver. And what exactly do you mean?"

"The name of my...*business*...is the Braided Crop Ranch. We're really a club, of sorts, with a resort hotel on the premises."

Hmm. "Oh. And you offer riding as part of the resort experience?"

Mr. Marsland laughed. "No. No riding. Only ponies."

"I'm sorry. I'm a bit confused about—"

"We're a fetish ranch, Oliver. Pony play. Human ponies. In leather harnesses and other...accoutrements."

I blinked quickly, my eyes flitting from the tomato to the glass of water on my desk as my mouth went dry.

"Oh. I see."

Holy... That was *not* where I thought this conversation was going. A fetish ranch? My mind conjured up bizarre images of people in horse costumes. I wasn't sure how I felt about that.

Adam laughed again. "Look, why don't I text you the link

to our website, where we have some older images, and you can call me back if you're interested. And just text me a 'No, thanks' if you're not."

That...made sense. My mind reeled from the information but also honed in razor-sharp on the fact that this would be a very different assignment from anything I'd done in the past.

"All right. That sounds fine."

"I hope to hear from you within the next hour. But if I don't, no harm, no foul. What we'd be looking for are updated, artistic images for the website and our brochures—maybe a selection of shots to sell in our gift shop. Have a look, and if you think you can work with us, call me back. At any rate, it was great to speak with you, Oliver."

"Same, Mr. Marsland."

"*Adam.* Please."

"Okay. Thanks, Adam. I've got your text, so I'll have a look."

"Excellent. Hope to speak to you soon."

I closed the call and clicked the link in the text from Adam. My browser opened, and a "Welcome" page loaded.

The Braided Crop Ranch scrolled in elegant but readable script overtop an idyllic scene of what looked like a regular farmhouse and barns in a woodland setting. Then a warning window popped up, informing me I had to be eighteen or older to enter the site.

Hmm. Well, I was thirty, so I clicked it.

WELCOME TO THE BRAIDED CROP RANCH.

A FETISH FARM FOR PONY PLAY ENTHUSIASTS...

And, okay, wow. I didn't even finish reading the intro because my eyes were drawn to the photos below it. Photos that turned my initial intrigue into outright fascination.

The images were pretty good, honestly, but a bit on the amateur side. Anyway, it wasn't the style of the photos that grabbed my attention, but their subjects.

I was no prude, and I had been involved in some fetish shoots in my time in this business. But those had been at cheesy, publicized events in the straight community, featuring stereotyped costuming and traditional BDSM props. It had been challenging to take photos that didn't reflect on that fact and didn't also sensationalize the subject matter.

But *this*...this looked like a pony play ranch for *boys.* Well, men, of course. But the word captioned on the images of these gorgeous young guys in very unique fetish-wear, was *ponyboys.*

I'd be lying if I said the word itself didn't send a thrill down my spine and straight to my tightening balls.

Holy fucking shit.

So this was the Braided Crop Ranch, where Adam Marsland wanted me to spend my summer photographing ponyboys, and all the things they got up to?

I spent a few more minutes examining the photos of naked men in leather harness, with full horsehair tails cascading from their asses, and shiny, steel cages on their penises. They were entrancing in their uniqueness and the edgy, casual way the kink was presented. They weren't trying to *be* horses. They were men submitting to being *treated* like horses. And that made all the difference.

Absolutely, I wanted to take photos of these pretty boys all summer at the Braided Crop Ranch. Who wouldn't? Especially because I *did* happen to be a gay man, and I couldn't imagine a more arousing spectacle than watching ponyboys prance around in the gear I'd seen.

I tapped my fingers on the desk, mind spinning, and body on high alert. Those photos were really doing it for me, and they weren't even that good. Imagine what *I* could produce.

I called Adam. He picked up after the first ring.

"Oliver. I'm so glad to hear from you."

I pulled my wheeled desk chair out and sat down.

"Adam, I've gone through the photos on the website. They aren't bad, but I could definitely produce something superior, especially if I have six weeks to follow some individual ponyboys around and document their daily activities."

When Adam replied, his voice was light and excited. He already seemed like a stand-up guy and I was already looking forward to working with him.

"Amazing! I was hoping you'd be interested. We'd have to ensure that no identifying features or marks were visible in the photos, of course. Privacy is a major concern for us here."

I picked up a pen and started to doodle on my gas bill. "Yeah, I wanted to talk to you about that. I'm willing to do this for you, Adam, but I'd like to publish the photos under a pseudonym."

"Of course. I don't have any issue with that."

I felt I had to explain. "I just don't know if I want to associate my professional name with this. I believe it's just as valuable a pursuit as any other type of photography, but I'm worried I'll lose out on other opportunities if someone less flexible sees that I take these kinds of photos, as well as the mainstream stuff."

"I completely understand," Adam replied.

The words I'd said didn't sit well with me. I ran a hand through my hair and walked over to the window. "I'm not ashamed to take photos of beautiful boys, Adam." I cleared my throat. "I assume they're all of legal age?"

"Yes, of course. We have a minimum age requirement of twenty to sign up as a ponyboy at the ranch. We don't think people younger than that have the mental maturity to handle the experience since it's so immersive."

"Okay. Good. Anyway, as I was saying, I'm not ashamed or embarrassed to do this work. Not at all. And those harnesses and the cages...I mean...*Jesus*. Do the ponyboys wear those things day-to-day?"

Adam chuckled softly. "They do. Almost every day."

I swallowed, my mouth suddenly dry. "Every...day? Okay, you've got to tell me. How does the Braided Crop Ranch function, exactly?"

"I'd rather explain that to you in person, Oliver. When you arrive in July." He paused. "All I can say is, four years into operations, the ranch works beautifully. I'd like you to come and make a photographic record of that."

If I passed this opportunity up? It would be a huge regret.

There wasn't any reason I could think of *not* to go.

"What sort of compensation are we talking about?" I asked, getting down to the nitty gritty. Perhaps I should have led with that. But my brain was blinded with pictures of pretty ponyboys, so...

We went over what Adam was willing to offer.

He'd house me, feed me, entertain me, as long as I took a good amount of photos and tried to make the ranch look as professional and exclusive and exciting as it really was. He also offered me enough money to make the venture worthwhile, even if I chose not to add the images to my professional portfolio. His confidence in the workings of his ranch was contagious, and by the end of the discussion, I was eager to see the place.

"All right. I'll do it." I said, tossing the pen across the table and rolling my chair back. *Fuck you, stupid red tomato.* I gave my computer the finger, grinning ear-to-ear.

"Fantastic," Adam said. "The summer session begins on the twelfth of July. The ponyboys will be arriving over the weekend and getting settled, so if you come on-site midweek, that would be perfect. It'll give me time to let everyone know you'll be wandering around taking photos, as long as they agree. Consent it very important at my ranch, even for something as seemingly benign as this. But I don't think we'll have a problem with a lack of participation. Most of the men who play pony here are very much into exhibitionism."

I could only fucking imagine. "Sure."

"When you arrive, I can give you a quick orientation and you can dive right in. That work for you?"

"Yes. That's fine."

"Text me your email address and I'll have Connor send out our standard welcome letter with attached directions and information. We usually send it to incoming staff, so just ignore the parts that aren't relevant."

"Sure. Thanks."

"I'll see you on July twelfth, Oliver. Thank you so much for agreeing to my request. Jaden couldn't say enough positive things about you."

"I'm glad he passed my name on. I'm looking forward to it."

We ended the call, and I texted Mr. Marsland my private email address.

*

I FOUND MYSELF unable to stop thinking about my summer contract. Time couldn't pass quickly enough, and when my planned assignment was a week away, I could hardly believe it.

"What do you mean?" My friend, Grif, said, when I explained that I'd be out of town for six weeks at an undisclosed location. "You're not going to one of these new-age monastic retreats, are you? You know they're all money-grabs, right?"

"Uh, no. That's not where I'm going. And I'm being paid well for my time."

He side-eyed me and sipped his beer. "Well, I just hope I eventually get the inside story. Seeing as I'm your best friend, I really do deserve to know where you're going. I assume you'll be reachable by cell?"

I hesitated. "Well..."

"Okay, come on. Where the fuck are you going and why is it a big secret?"

"Fine. But I need you to keep quiet because I'm doing this assignment under the radar since it's a little out of the mainstream."

Grif's eyebrows flew up. He was older than me by a couple of years but still looked like he was twenty-five. He didn't have any trouble getting laid, and he thought I was overplaying my concern at turning thirty. But I didn't have the genes to look boyish my entire life like Grif apparently did. I was starting to get lines beside my mouth and eyes—barely visible so far but they were there—and I'd already found a couple of grey hairs

I thought for second. "Actually, it's way out of the mainstream. And I don't know if I want my professional name associated with this."

Grif sat up straighter. "Now I'm going to die if you don't tell me."

"You're not going to die."

"But you're going to tell me, right?"

I tapped my fingers on the wood of the tabletop and smiled, staring at the varnished surface and wondering if telling Grif was a good idea or a bad one. I knew he'd keep it a secret if it killed him, but knowing Grif, this secret might just kill him.

"I'm going to be photographing men at a kinky pony play ranch in the Muskokas," I said.

Grif stared at my profile silently for a few seconds. Then he slammed his beer down so hard, the liquid sloshed over the sides.

"What?"

"Shh, *Jesus*, this is supposed to be a secret."

"Did you just say—"

"Kinky ponyboys at a ranch in Northern Ontario. Yeah. That's what I said."

"Ponyboys?" He whispered, grey eyes glinting dangerously, breaths becoming ragged. "*Ponyboys!*"

"Griffin, are you having an asthma attack?"

"Maybe? I can't breathe all of a sudden. Are you fucking kidding me?"

"No, I'm completely serious. You know I'm a photographer."

"*How?* How did you finagle this? And why didn't you tell me sooner?"

I narrowed my eyes at him. "You can't come with me."

"Even just to visit?"

"I won't have my phone most of the time."

"I can't even *call* you?"

"I'll have it, I just have to leave it in my room at the main house. So, I can call *you*, on occasion."

He stared at me. "You better fucking call me. I'm going to want to know every fucking thing you do there."

"I'm just taking pictures, Grif." I shrugged. "That's all."

He sat back in his chair, regarding me quizzically. "Apparently, you're going to live at this—ranch?—for six weeks. Maybe you won't just take pictures."

"What?"

"You're telling me, you're going to spend your days photographing half-naked, kinky men, playing pony for sexual kicks, and that's it?"

I nodded. "Yeah. You know I'm a professional. I can be professional at a kink ranch just like anyplace else."

He seemed dubious.

"I'm not going for pleasure, Grif. I'm going on a professional assignment."

"So, you're not going to get any pleasure from taking intimate photos of naked men in the pony barn? Wearing bridles and harnesses, and who knows what-the-fuck else, and you're not going to get *anything* from that?"

I levelled a meaningful stare his way.

"I'm sure that— Look, I'm obviously going to enjoy this. What gay guy wouldn't?"

"Uh-huh."

"But it will be a vicarious enjoyment, because I'm going to be there as a professional photographer, not a member of this very exclusive fetish club. I'm going to have to keep a professional distance in order to do my job properly."

"If you say so." Grif took a gulp of his beer, put it down, and laughed softly. "Wow. I'm actually thrilled for you, Ollie.

Sounds like an incredible way to spend your summer."

I grinned, lifting my beer. "Let's drink to that. And not a word to anyone about where I am. Just say you don't know, that I needed a vacation, and I didn't tell you where I was going."

"Of course. I can keep a secret. But you have to promise you'll call me and let me know what it's like."

"Fine."

He clinked his glass with mine, and we drank to half-naked, kinky men, and a secret, summer retreat.

*

I DIDN'T KNOW what to pack.

Adam had said the summers were hot, dry and sunny, and to bring shorts, boots and flip-flops, comfortable cotton shirts, and a few nicer pieces to wear to the communal suppers and the annual Canada Day bonfire. I also might want to go off-site to the bars and restaurants in Huntsville on occasion, or the resort hotel attached to the ranch.

But I'd never had to prepare for such an unusual assignment before, and I found myself wanting to bring clothes that made me look not only professional, but...*hot*. I would be taking pictures of incredibly good-looking young men (if the photos already on the website were anything to go by) for six weeks. Even though I planned to maintain a professional distance from my subjects, I wanted them to think I was a passably attractive man.

I'd hit the ripe old age of thirty several months ago, and it had taken some of the wind out of my sails, to be honest. True, it wasn't that old. And I had been able to make a good name for myself in the business of digital photography. I was established and rarely had to go looking for work anymore, which was a huge accomplishment at my age.

But as a gay guy, I hated to admit there was a stigma about men in their thirties—that we weren't any fun anymore—that we were over the hill. I felt stuck in an in-between land of gay stereotypes. I was too old to be a twink but too young to be a Daddy.

I know, I know, it was ridiculous to think in terms like that, but I couldn't help it. My social feed was full of posing twenty-somethings who'd throw out offhand comments about gay men over thirty, and it...stung.

Maybe the problem was who I followed on Twitter and Instagram—largely, men who were younger than thirty. So, yeah, maybe I had a thing for cute twinks with biteable asses and an affinity for drama. And it hurt that maybe they wouldn't be attracted to me anymore, because I'd reached the expiry date for fellow twinkdom but wasn't yet "Daddy" material. Even though I felt like a "Daddy" most of the time, since I'd become responsible and predictable due to my entrepreneurial business and need to earn an actual living.

I'd be the first to say those preconceptions and assumptions were unfair. But it still seemed they existed.

Anyway, I ended up with one suitcase and my camera bag, both of which I stuffed in the trunk of my eight-year-old Toyota, before locking up my house and heading to the highway for the two-and-half-hour drive to the Braided Crop Ranch on Skeleton Lake. In exchange for occasional bits of information from my secret mission, Grif had agreed to look after my house and feed my fish every few days.

I'd jacked off twice the night before to the photos on the website. So yeah, I was excited to observe the ponyboys at the Braided Crop Ranch in person. But I wondered how long my professional distance would hold once I found myself deep in the world of kinky pony play.

CHAPTER TWO

A REVEALING ORIENTATION

OR

HOW MUCH LUBE DOES A PONY PLAY RANCH NEED?

I PULLED INTO the parking lot of the main house at the Braided Crop Ranch at one forty-five on Wednesday, July twelfth, after buzzing through at the gate.

By this time, I was practically salivating to get my eyes on an in-the-flesh ponyboy. It had taken almost three months for this opportunity to manifest, and I couldn't wait to start taking pictures.

As I slid my car into a parking spot—there were only a handful of vehicles in the dirt-covered lot—the front door opened and a well-dressed, dark-haired, man came out to wave to me.

Adam.

I turned off the engine and stepped out of the car, glad to be able to stretch my legs and almost vibrating with anticipation. The noise of cicadas filled my ears as the July sun burned down on me, and I wondered if I should have brought some kind of hat. Adam had said they took the ponyboys outside as often as they could when the weather was fair.

I looked up to see the man walking toward me and barely had time to acknowledge to myself how attractive he was, in an old-world, fifties-movie-star way, before he offered his hand for me to shake.

"Oliver. Welcome to the Braided Crop Ranch! We're so glad to have you join us," Adam Marsland stated in an affable tenor. I felt eminently welcomed by his beaming smile.

I shook his hand and matched his grin. "Great to finally meet you, Adam." I gazed up at the large modern farmhouse with generous windows and cheerful paint. "So this is the Braided Crop Ranch."

Adam laughed. "This is the parking lot and the main house—the most boring and utilitarian parts of the BCR. But we'll start there. You can get settled in your room and I'll take you for an orientation around the grounds."

"I'm looking forward to that," I said, rubbing my forehead where sweat had gathered already and squinting in the sunshine.

"Did you bring a hat? You may be outside quite a bit."

"Uh, that's one thing I forgot. I'm sure there's more. But I brought all my camera equipment, which is the important thing," I said as we walked up the steps.

Adam opened the door for me. "I can grab you a ball cap from the gift shop."

"Sure."

Gift shop? This place seemed to have everything. Naked men playing pony, beautiful scenery, nice lodgings, and a gift shop. Colour me impressed.

The entry opened up to a bright hallway that reminded me of the bottom floor of an office building—polished and utilitarian.

"Stay here. I'll be right back," Adam said, putting a friendly hand on my shoulder briefly and then moving down the hall to the left of me. I noticed a young man, whose disembodied voice had no doubt buzzed me in, at a desk to the right, speaking in low tones on a desk phone. He waved to me with a smile that I returned, then kept talking into the phone and typing on his computer.

I noticed that the ambient temperature in here, where my accommodations were to be, was much more comfortable than outside, which meant they had central air in this building. Thank goodness.

Adam returned and handed me a navy-blue ball cap with *BCR* embroidered across the front in swirly red script. "This should do for now."

"Thanks," I said, taking it from him. My first souvenir.

"Come and meet Connor," Adam said, leading me down the hall.

Connor replaced the phone receiver and stood, giving me another smile and offering his hand. "Hi, Oliver."

"Connor," I said, shaking his hand. He looked to be in his mid-twenties and wore a pair of chinos and a short-sleeved, white button-down.

"How was the drive?" he asked.

I shrugged. "Long and boring, but okay."

"You didn't get lost?"

"No. Your instructions were excellent." I glanced at

Adam. "You've got the perfect, secluded set-up, here."

"You haven't even seen the best parts of our ranch, Oliver," Adam interjected. "Why don't you get settled in your room? Connor can help you bring your equipment in." He reached over Connor's desk and grabbed something, passing me a room key. "Number eight, on the second floor."

"Thanks." I adjusted the strap on the ball cap so it fit snugly.

"I'll be in my office." He gestured to an open door behind Connor's area. "Come and get me when you're ready for your walkabout. I'm excited to show you how the ranch works and why it's so special. You won't need your camera. I want you to get a feel for things before you start."

"Sure."

Connor came around and we walked outside to my car. I opened the trunk and hauled out my suitcase. "If you don't mind carrying this, I can bring the camera equipment."

"Sure," Connor said.

I brought out the large canvas tote bag containing my cameras, lenses, and tripod and shut the trunk, making sure the car was locked, even though I was confident they didn't get many people wandering through here without an invitation. There wasn't much in my car to steal.

"How long have you worked at the BCR, Connor?" I asked.

He followed me up the front steps.

"It's been a couple of years now."

"Adam seems like a great guy."

"He's amazing. The ranch is amazing. You'll like it here. The trainers are awesome and the ponyboys are so much fun."

I grinned. "I can't wait to see them in action."

"Yeah, I don't think you're prepared for what you're going to see, honestly. I don't think anyone would be." He laughed, and his cheeks flushed.

We carried the bags up to my room, and Connor helped put them inside.

"This looks very comfortable. Thanks, Connor."

"No problem. You'll probably run into Kamal and Lorraine and some of the other trainers when they're not working, since they have rooms on this floor. But everyone should be very welcoming. We know you're here to take photos, and we're all excited about that." He smiled. "Some of us may have googled you."

I laughed. "I would expect no less."

"You take incredibly sexy pictures of fruit. I can't wait to see what you do with the ponyboys."

"Thanks," I said, shrugging. "It's a living."

I hefted my duffel bag onto the bed and unzipped it, taking out my gear and checking to make sure everything was as it should be. There was a spot in the corner by the dresser, where I could stash the tripod, and I put the expensive camera gear out on one end of the dresser so it was easily accessible. I plugged in the cord for my laptop and set it to charge beside where my phone was already set up on the side table. Adam had said that I could keep it, but it had to stay in my room at all times. Nobody was permitted out of the main house with a cell phone. Apparently, the ponyboys had their devices confiscated upon entry and kept in a locked cabinet, only useable for brief periods upon request.

This ranch must be something special, for people to relinquish their technology in such a way.

I had to piss and was impressed by the cleanliness and finishes in the full bathroom. There was a walk-in shower, toilet, vanity and modern sink, as well as a medicine cabinet. Utilitarian but also pretty. Better than the one I had at home that desperately needed updating.

I glanced at myself in the mirror. The ball cap made me look younger than thirty, so I figured I'd keep using it, although I'd have to swing it around while taking photos, or even remove it. It was soft enough I could stuff it in my back pocket if needed and the brim flipped up too. I looked even younger when I turned it around, so, yeah, that was a bonus. I might be halfway through my thirty-first year but I was damn well gonna channel some youthful energy during this assignment.

Not that I wanted to hook up. I needed to keep things professional. But that didn't mean I didn't want to present a tempting option for these kinky ponyboys. It would be an ego boost to be the sexy, talented photographer they all wanted but couldn't have.

LOL. As if.

I shook my head at my reflection. Was there any end to my narcissistic delusions?

Downstairs, I nodded to Connor and knocked on Adam's open door.

"You ready?" he asked.

"I think so," I grinned. "Probably not. But I'd better get a glimpse into life at the Braided Crop Ranch so I can formulate an action plan."

We headed the other way down the hall, past what looked like a cafeteria, to a door at the back, which Adam pushed open onto a wide, wrap-around porch.

"Wow," I said as we stepped out. Green grass stretched ahead of us, bordered by thick forest and interspersed with several wood structures.

"This is it," Adam said.

"It's beautiful. What a perfect spot for a—I mean, holy shit."

We walked across the porch and down the three steps.

"I'll take you to the grooming barn, first. You can see the space where our stable hands prepare the ponyboys."

My mouth went dry. "Okay."

As we crossed the first stretch of grass to a large, square building, my eyes were drawn to distant figures in one of the paddocks. I couldn't distinguish anything but movement and the number of people, which seemed to be three.

"Looks like one of the trainers has ponyboys outside already," Adam said. He pointed to a door on one end of the wooden structure marked PONIES. "This is where the ponyboys go to get undressed and ready for the session." He pulled open the door and gestured for me to enter.

I stepped into something reminiscent of a gym changing area. One wall was lined with lockers and long benches, and hooks for bags or wet coats. Three pairs of shoes were left undone on one of the benches—a set of dusty red chucks, a pair of brown Blundstones and some orange flip-flops, presumably belonging to the ponyboys in action this morning.

"There are two sessions per day. One in the morning and another in the afternoon. Ponyboys are assigned to one or the other each week," Adam explained. He gestured for me to follow him around a short wall to the other side of the grooming barn, where I was brought up short by the sight of three showerheads over a tiled floor space.

"Whoa," I said. "Jesus."

My eyes were drawn to the rubber wrist cuffs hanging above each one.

"They're bound in here? Naked?" I said, mouth dry, and brain already processing images of water-soaked flesh.

Adam nodded. "Oh, yes. It helps get them into the submissive headspace they need for their training sessions. They become ponies being groomed, rather than people taking showers."

"I see." Or rather, I *would* see. And I would take photos of the ponyboys from the moment they stepped out of the changing area to the moment they went back to it, if I was permitted.

I tore my eyes from the shower area. "I'll be able to

photograph them in here?"

He nodded. "In this section, yes. Not in the changing space."

"Sure. Of course."

The finishes were high-end. The larger room looked like a strange sort of spa or physio clinic, with a wall of cupboards and drawers, a large table strewn with harnesses and other gear in the midst of being cleaned, and a large whiteboard with names and what looked like instructions scrawled in black marker.

The door at the other end of the building opened and a woman with red hair in a ponytail came inside. She was a tiny thing, and not what I expected to see in the grooming barn at a gay ponyplay ranch.

"Hey Adam," she beamed.

"Liv," Adam said, "I wondered where everybody was."

"Sorry. I had to get some more supplies." She had an armful of bottles. "You know, we really need to put this stuff on tap or something."

Adam laughed. "That's not a bad idea."

She threw me a grin and her eyes flashed with intelligence. "You must be Oliver. Welcome to the Braided Crop Ranch."

I moved forward and extended my hand. "That's me."

"Nice hat."

"Thanks. I forgot to bring one."

"Hold on, I'm juggling a hundred bottles of lube." She dropped them onto the table, making sure none rolled off, and took my hand. "Did you just arrive?"

"Yes. Adam's showing me around."

Liv was dressed in Lycra shorts and a tank top, with pink flip-flops on her small feet. Her toes were painted a vibrant shade of orange.

"Oliver's going to start photographing the ponyboys tomorrow," Adam said, "But I want him to get a feel for the light and the spaces he'll be working with."

"Nice. Sounds like a sweet gig." She waggled her eyebrows.

I laughed, immediately warming to her. "Yeah. Seems like."

"He hasn't seen a ponyboy up close, yet," Adam said.

"Lorraine has Puck and Justin in the paddock. I think Michael's got the morning off?"

"Yes, he had an appointment. Perfect. I'll be taking Oliver over there. Hiro's working with Andrew in the arena?"

Liv nodded. "Yep."

I glanced at the whiteboard, seeing the names Andrew, Justin, and Puck at the top of each column.

"The trainers write down what gear they want their ponyboys to be wearing when presented to them at the start of their shift," Adam explained. "It varies from day-to-day, although the body harnesses, collars and cock cages are standard. It's up to the trainers if they want extras."

I swallowed thickly. "Extras?"

Liv chuckled. "Bridles, tails, masks. It depends. The first pony show is on Saturday, but it's pretty basic. The ponyboys don't wear full gear in the shows at the beginning. Full tack takes getting used to."

Full. Tack. What did that even mean? My head swam with questions.

"So, the men are put under the showerheads," I said, trying to understand fully. "Bound, so they get into the submissive headspace," I glanced at Adam. "And then, what? Just washed? Or...are there other preparations?"

I didn't feel like blurting out "Do you give them enemas?" even though that was what I wanted to know.

"There are douching kits in the bunkhouse, that they can use before they arrive at the grooming barn," Adam said, perching himself on one corner of the large wooden table.

"We decided it would be too messy and invasive to do that here. Although we did consider it at one point."

I nodded and Liv placed a hand on her chest. "From the bottom of my heart, I thank you, Adam."

Adam winked at her. "You kids work hard enough without having to do all that as well. And the men probably prefer to do it in relative privacy. Although it might make for an even more debasing experience if it was done in the grooming barn. It was more a matter of timing and hygiene, really. I wouldn't have any objections other than those two."

"You are so pragmatic, Adam," Liv rolled her eyes.

He inclined his head.

"So, what are we going to do with the photographs Oliver will be taking?" she said, standing the bottles of lube in an organized way on the table.

He shrugged. "Well, I want to update the website. And *Dark Horse Magazine* wants to do a feature spread on the Braided Crop Ranch."

"No shit! That's amazing!" Liv grinned and me and gave me a thumbs up.

"I...don't know what that means," I said. I'd never heard of *Dark Horse Magazine.*

"*Dark Horse Magazine* is a leading American fetish

publication. We're hoping a feature can increase our reach. Right now, we're largely word of mouth. It would be nice to have more guys coming up from the States." Adam stood. "They would normally send a photographer of their own, but I told them that might not be necessary, that we had someone coming to take professional shots of the ranch. I thought perhaps they could use some of your images, but only if you're comfortable with it. You'd receive the standard royalties if the magazine prints them. We can look over the contract they've emailed me."

"Something to think about, for sure. I don't mind, really, as long as they agree to use my alias in the publication."

"I'm sure that won't be a problem. I don't want more than one photographer on the ranch at a time. I'm hoping that having you taking your images won't disrupt the day-to-day operations too much. The last thing I want to do is take the ponyboys out of the headspace they're in. The more you can make your task fit into the fantasy of pony play, the better."

I cleared my throat. "Pardon?"

Adam laughed. "I just mean that while you're taking your photos you'll need to buy in to the fact that these men want to be seen as ponies when they are in harness. Whether they're posing for you or they're in the grooming barn getting bathed and polished, try not to invade that headspace with real-world matters."

Ah.

"I think I can do that. Do they have pony names, or do I call them by their actual names?"

"They do have pony names, but those are only used in the show ring. The trainers use their real first names, and you can as well. It makes things easier for everyone, and then it's a kick to use their pony names in the shows."

"Sure."

I was beginning to realize the Braided Crop Ranch was a complex and intricate haven for dedicated fetish enthusiasts, designed and run for their benefit so they could fulfill their fantasies in a safe space.

Adam stood. "Let's go. I'm sure Liv has work to do, and I need to introduce you to some trainers."

"Sure."

"Bye, Oliver," Liv said. "Have fun! I wish I could be introduced to this place all over again. It's a trip!"

On the short walk to the next, larger outbuilding, I asked Adam about having a female stable hand.

He glanced at me. "You may be surprised to learn we have a female trainer working here."

"Really?" Connor had mentioned someone named Lorraine, and I was definitely curious.

"Yes. Because what the ponyboys do here isn't entirely sexual. It's more about being handled and used and asked to perform difficult tasks for the reward of serving their master. Yes, there are some basic sexual rewards and sometimes punishments, but most of this is about dominance, submission, and service."

By this time, we'd reached the door to the arena, and Adam grabbed the handle. "You ready, Oliver?"

"Fuck, Adam. Yes, I'm ready."

He was killing me.

He smiled and pulled open the door.

"Hold your head up!" echoed across the polished wood floors as we stepped inside and Adam closed the door.

My eyes adjusted slowly to the fractured light as the sounds of boots pounding in a steady rhythm filled the space.

"Good afternoon, Hiro." Adam addressed a thick-set man in jodhpurs, tall brown boots, and a white button-down, with thick black hair and the sliver of a mustache. "How is Andrew doing today?"

As we approached Hiro, his eyes scanned me with curiosity before he smiled at Adam. "Very well for a new recruit.

He has a fine form for only his third shift. And I can tell he's trying."

While they spoke, I examined the large, indoor area. Natural light from a border of windows directly beneath the ceiling all the way around helped illuminate the space, but there was tinting to keep out any direct beams, which would make it ideal for creating optimal images.

"Hiro, this is Oliver, our resident photographer," Adam said, while my gaze was drawn to the figure moving nearby. "Oliver, I've let all the trainers know you'll be on site and taking photographs for the next six weeks."

A slim but muscular young man with shoulder-length red hair and an abundance of freckles covering his pale skin, jogged near the outer wall. He wore the body harness and collar I'd seen in the images on the website, as well as the leather forearm cuffs that kept his arms pinioned at his back. His feet, in black Doc Martin boots, struck the floor in measured beats as he tried to keep his head up, maintain his momentum, and avoid falling.

"Welcome to the ranch, Oliver," Hiro said.

I tore my eyes away from the ponyboy and smiled at the man who stood a little shorter than both Adam and I.

"Thanks. I'm pleased to meet you, Hiro." I shook his

offered hand. Then my gaze flew back to Andrew.

"This is the first time he's seen a ponyboy in actuality," Adam said.

"Oh? Well, then, let's give you a closer look." He clapped his hands. "Andrew! Come here and stand for our visitors, please."

My mouth went dry as the ponyboy jogged over and came to a stop before his trainer.

Andrew's athletic body shone with sweat and glowed with exertion. His chest rose and fell under the leather of his harness as he caught his breath.

"Good boy," Hiro said, "This is Oliver. He's going to be taking photos of you and the other ponyboys over the next six weeks while we put you through your paces."

Andrew turned his soft-eyed gaze to me, and I scrambled for any kind of appropriate response.

"Hi, Andrew," I said, trying not to stare at his small, flaccid prick in its steel cage and the line of red hair leading down his middle to where his pubes had been trimmed neatly.

Andrew glanced briefly at Hiro, who nodded, before answering, "Hi, Oliver."

Holy shit. This was already a total mindfuck. Andrew seemed to assess me for a moment, and then his gaze settled on his trainer.

"You've done well today, Andrew," Hiro said, tousling the man's mop of red hair and prompting a relieved expression.

"He looks great," Adam concurred. "Are you keeping him out of the sun?"

"Yeah," Hiro admitted, "His pretty pale skin burns too easily. But I'll try to get him out there when the sun isn't so high and strong."

"Good idea. You can ask the stable hands to put extra strong sunscreen on him, too."

"I will."

"I'm going to take Oliver to meet Lorraine and the other ponyboys," Adam said, laying a hand briefly on Hiro's shoulder and then leading me to another door at the side of the arena.

I followed, glancing back a couple of times to see Hiro speaking softly to Andrew while the ponyboy nodded and shrugged, his breathing seeming to regulate after the short rest.

Maybe it was because I'd never understood the hoopla about redheads. Andrew's pale, freckled skin and rust-coloured body hair didn't do anything for me. Sure, he was good-looking, but nothing about his appearance, except for the pony-play accoutrements, interested me in the least.

The leather harness and the armbands, the cock in the cage, the submissive manner, all reinforced the kinky aspect of this roleplay. Although Andrew was attractive, and his body, restrained in such a manner, certainly titillated me, I couldn't help feeling slightly disappointed in a strange way.

I'd been half-expecting someone stunningly beautiful and powerful, restrained before a strict and intimidating trainer, when Andrew seemed decidedly normal, and Hiro, though he affected an authority I couldn't deny, really didn't seem all that threatening.

Well, I'd been building all of it up in my head for months, so it wasn't that surprising my first ponyboy hadn't measured up to my expectations. And since I wasn't new to kink entirely, the strangeness of seeing a man bound in leather was less than it might be for a total neophyte.

As we headed out the other door, back into the warmth of the day, I wondered if nothing at the BCR would measure up to my high expectations, and I'd have to disguise my disappointment with enthusiastic photography. No doubt, I'd be able to capture the ponyboys in such a way as to emphasize the strangeness and uniqueness of their position and the tantalizing nature of their subservience enough to satisfy even the most casual observer, even if I wasn't as taken with it as I'd expected.

CHAPTER THREE

PUCK

OR

A DISGRUNTLED PADDOCK PONY

I FOLLOWED ADAM over the grass to the paddock, where a diminutive, brown-haired woman in jeans and a green-flecked blouse led a tall ponyboy by his leather harness. The man's sweat-slicked skin gleamed like oil-soaked leather, and his features seemed modelled after ancient Egyptian gods.

The unexpected let-down I'd felt after getting a close look

at Andrew faded, now I was presented with *this* ponyboy in his gear.

That's more like it.

I heard the jingle of metal and turned toward the other ponyboy in the paddock. In a moment, all thoughts of Andrew and the majestic, brown-skinned man left me.

Tied to the fence of the paddock by a rough rope looped into the ring of his wide leather collar, *this* ponyboy regarded me with a disdain. His vivid green eyes pinned me with animosity, as if he owned the ranch and I was an annoying interloper.

"Looks like Puck needs another attitude adjustment," Adam said. "Oh look, here comes Kamal."

Puck seemed to start at this information, his demeanor changing. He tore his aggressive gaze off me and stared at the ground, where his scuffed boots were planted a shoulder length apart in the dirt. I took a moment to scan Puck's restrained form and found my mouth pooling with saliva. He was delicious and exactly to my tastes.

"Adam. Who's this?" The baritone voice came from behind me.

As Adam replied with my name and the reason I was here, I examined the swarthy older man. Ruggedly attractive, with salt-and-pepper hair and olive skin, what struck me most was the man's absolute authority in this paddock.

He assessed me, then held out his hand. "Oliver. Glad to have you at the ranch. I see Adam's already got you decked out in official BCR merchandise."

"Oliver forgot to bring a hat," Adam said.

"*You're* not wearing a hat," Kamal pointed out. "And neither am I."

Adam raised his brows. "You're just as oppositional as Puck. Maybe Oliver doesn't want to end up with a sunburn on his first day."

Kamal smiled, his face the picture of affability. "I dabble in photography myself."

"Do you?" I said politely, although the number of times I'd had people say this to me and then shown me some very amateurish photos was considerable. I felt I should give this charismatic man the benefit of the doubt.

"Well, it's a hobby. I might want to bend your ear once or twice."

"Sure."

"How has Puck been this morning?" Adam asked. "He seemed a bit peeved when we arrived."

"He's annoyed because I decided to pay attention to

Justin instead of him," Lorraine said. The other trainer had come close with the majestic dark ponyboy. She was stunning at this range, with a diamond stud in her pert nostril and a composure almost as authoritative as Kamal's.

"Lorraine, this is Oliver Lambert. Our resident photographer for the summer."

Lorraine offered her delicate hand. "Oliver, welcome."

She turned to Kamal. "That hotblood is begging for a punishment of some kind. He's been nothing but saucy all morning. I thought tying him to the fence might help, but he can't seem to settle."

Kamal gazed at where the black-haired ponyboy stood stiffly by the fence.

"He looks all right now."

Adam chuckled. "Only because you're here. You should have seen the look he threw poor Oliver!"

Puck's shoulders stiffened, and his hands became fists as he stared at the ground like he wanted to murder it.

What had made him so angry? Surely, he was here for the pony play. Did he not like his trainer?

"Hotblood?" I asked. "Is that a horse term?"

Lorraine nodded. "Yes. It refers to the smaller, more high-strung breeds, like Arabians and Thoroughbreds.

Gorgeous creatures but they can wear you out a bit."

Kamal chuckled. "Puck's a bit of a drama queen. And he likes to back talk. See how quiet he is now? He knows what I've brought for him."

Kamal held up an item that made my knees go weak when I thought about what he was about to do with it. It was a ponytail plug, like the ones I'd seen in the website photos. Thick and solid, with waves of black horsehair cascading down from the flange, the object at once utilitarian and intimidating.

"Ah," Adam said. "I see."

Puck's head swivelled and his gaze locked on the tail. He shook his head and tried to move away, but the rope attaching him to the fence prevented his escape.

"Calm down," Kamal said, moving toward him. "You don't want an audience? You should have thought of that when you cursed at me earlier, when all I did was criticize your gait. You want to be a pony at the BCR, Puck? You need to watch your tongue when you're with me. I don't abide rude behaviour, and I told you that on your first day." Kamal's voice, though stern, didn't carry any aggression, simply imparting the cold facts to the recalcitrant young man.

Kamal gazed at Puck, then me, then Adam. "Can I

borrow Oliver?"

Adam raised his eyebrows at me and shrugged. "If it's okay with him."

I gave Kamal a half smile, wondering what he wanted me to do.

"Perfect," Kamal said. "Come over here."

I moved forward and stopped where Kamal indicated. He walked to where Puck's rope wrapped around the fence pole and untied him, speaking softly to him while he did it. Puck gave a pert nod, then a shake of his head, as Kamal held onto the rope at his collar and led him to me.

Those eyes shot lightning bolts, as if all Puck wanted was to smite me into the dirt. He frowned, his lips in a scowl, as Kamal brought him over and passed me the rope.

"Hold him."

I froze. "Um..."

"Just hold the rope, Oliver."

I exchanged a glance with Kamal and took the rope, grabbing it lower down. Puck was free to move if he wanted to. But he stayed where he was and burned lasers into me as I stood, confused and aroused before him.

We were a similar height. He was fucking glorious.

Sleek muscles coated with sweat, his fair skin spattered

here-and-there with dark-brown moles that only proved how unblemished and perfect he was otherwise. His sweat-damp hair curled against his head with casual abandon, framing a Grecian face—full lips, aristocratic nose, and high cheek bones.

He had a barbell in his left eyebrow and right nipple, and a silver ring circling his bottom lip. He looked like one of the club kids from home, captured in this rural environment and out-of-his-depth. I'd lay wages Puck was an out-and-out city boy.

I tried to focus on anything but how ethereal this young man looked in his pony gear, because my heart was fucking breaking, and I'd only been here an hour. And Kamal was speaking.

"He'll have to bend over. Can you support his shoulders, Oliver?"

What?

"Pardon?"

Kamal stared at me and smiled slowly, like he knew exactly why I was distracted in this moment. He put a hand on my shoulder.

"Oliver."

"Yes?"

"I know he's fucking pretty. And I know you haven't been on the ranch very long. But I think it will help you with your photography if you get used to being up close and personal with Puck here. And I want Puck to have to suffer the indignity of having the resident professional photographer watch closely as he receives his ponytail for the very first time."

My mouth went dry, and I nodded, not daring to defy Kamal, and also understanding that I might as well wade into the deep end. I was here for the experience and to learn everything I could about being a ponyboy at the BCR, so I could capture it with my lens.

"Yes. Of course," I said, finding myself the object of Kamal's firm gaze after this unusual request.

Puck's chest rose and fell as he absorbed our conversation and seemed to become even more agitated. I think he hated me, but I couldn't worry about that right now, except to contemplate how unfair it was.

"Put your hands on his shoulders, so he can lean into you," Kamal said.

I faced Puck head-on and reached for his quivering shoulders. As I placed my open palms gently but firmly on him, he sighed and shook his head back and forth with exaggerated movements.

"Prospero," he said gruffly, turning to Kamal. "*Prospero.*"

"Drop your hands, Oliver," Kamal said and moved in close, gazing at Puck's bent head as Puck licked his lips over and over.

"What's happening?" I asked Adam, stepping back as Kamal whispered something into Puck's ear. "Did I do something wrong?"

"No, but I think Puck just used his safeword," Adam said.

"Oh," I said. *Because of me?*

Adam shrugged, watching Kamal and Puck speaking in hushed tones. "It happens. We don't really want them upset. They're able to back out at any point. They don't, usually. But sometimes they feel overwhelmed, and that's fair."

We watched as Kamal said a few more words, then went behind Puck and began to unbuckle the ponyboy's armbands.

"He's done for the day," Kamal said, with no animosity in his tone, only mild disappointment. He finished his task and let Puck bring his arms down.

The ponyboy was still frowning. He didn't seem any happier. He flexed his fingers and stretched his arms.

"You all right, Puck?" Kamal asked him.

"Yeah. I'm fine. I'm sorry," the man mumbled.

"Sorry for using your safeword, or sorry for being a pain in the ass?"

Puck glanced at me, and he seemed to think something over. "Sorry for everything. I'm not ready to be done. Not yet."

"Puck, it's fine. You safeworded. You're off the hook," Kamal assured him. "The stable hands will look after you."

"No. I'm fine!" He glared at Kamal. "I want you to"—his gaze flicked to me briefly as he spoke between clenched teeth—"give me the tail."

Kamal stared at Puck for several tense moments.

So long, in fact, that Adam, who had been careful to stay out of things, intervened. "Puck, it's all right. You're not a failure for using your safeword. You can start fresh tomorrow."

Kamal held up his hand. "No. If Puck wants to start fresh right now, that's his choice. We still have an hour."

Puck nodded, his face the picture of relief.

"Not good enough," Kamal stated.

"Yes. Please. I want it." Puck turned around and crossed his arms behind his back.

"Never mind that," Kamal said. "You can keep your arms free for the rest of your shift. If you're serious about continuing, go and lean on the fence over there. Stick out your ass and come up with a nice apology for Oliver and Adam after we're done."

Puck seemed to think it over. He gazed at me and then Adam, nodded and walked, subdued, to the fence.

Kamal watched him go, turned to Adam and me, and shrugged.

"Oliver, if you don't mind, I want Puck to see you while I do this. His attitude was out of line. Go around to the other side of the fence and stand in front of him."

I looked at Adam, raising my eyebrows.

Adam bumped me with his elbow. "I'd do what Kamal is asking if I were you."

My cheeks flushed, and I made my way to the outside of the fence, opposite to where Puck stood with his hands braced on the third rung, back arched and bottom pushed out for Kamal. He still had the armbands on and they made him look like some kind of rock star or motorcycle freak. Except that he was naked in a body harness and a cock cage and dusty black boots.

He wouldn't have looked out of place on an eighties Mad Max set.

I noticed, for the first time, his half-swollen penis

straining against the steel of the cage. I fixed on that image, wishing I had my camera so I could capture it properly. When my gaze drifted upwards, it was to find Puck staring at me.

This time, he wasn't scowling. Now he regarded me with a frank curiosity and seemed resigned to the fact I'd be observing his punishment. My dick twitched at the look in his eyes.

Uncomfortable and not sure what to do with myself, I took off my baseball cap and ran a hand through my hair, then turned the hat around and put it on backwards.

Kamal approached Puck and landed a rough smack on his backside, making him startle and shut his eyes. When he opened them they blazed fire, but not with anger. No, this was lust and a desperate hunger my body recognized. My pants felt too snug and I tried not to squirm under that heated gaze.

"Spread your legs, ponyboy," Kamal said.

Puck breathed heavily and obeyed, gaze still locked with mine.

"Wider."

When the ponyboy's boots were spread wide, Kamal smoothed a hand along Puck's flank, grabbing a black latex or nytril glove out of his back pocket and pulling it on with an aggressive snap. The sound made Puck jerk but he held his position. Kamal picked up a bottle of lube from beside the fence.

My overwhelmed brain swirled with questions. Where had the lube come from? Did the trainers stash lube everywhere it might possibly be needed? My gaze alternately focused on Puck's face and shifted to observe what Kamal was up to behind him.

Instead of hostility, Puck's eyes conveyed a certain vague interest in me, perhaps curiosity as to what I thought I was doing, coming onto this ranch to take photos of him and the other ponyboys. That was the impression I got. Or maybe he was simply curious about my reaction to what would happen in three, two, one...

Puck's eyes closed and he tossed his head. I could see Kamal's arm moving roughly as he used his gloved fingers to prepare the ponyboy for the large plug. I tried not to imagine what that would look like from Kamal's viewpoint–what it would feel like to have two or three fingers knuckle deep in this man.

Puck's breaths came heavy and his cheeks flushed. I had some experience with anal pleasure, and I'd played around with a few toys, as well, so I had a good idea how a plug that large would feel.

I'd never tried one with a ponytail attached to it but, hey, never say never.

I kept my gaze fixed on Puck's closed eyes as my brain conjured up all kinds of images. When they snapped open, and he locked on me with blown pupils as his lips parted with a stuttered moan, I thought I might mess my pants.

This was what I'd expected from my introduction to the BCR. I'd found it. I'd found *him*. The perfect fucking ponyboy of my fantasies. I only had six weeks, but that was enough time to try to get to know Puck, take lots of photos of him in all kinds of ponyboy predicaments, and take home enough spank-bank material to tide me over for a while.

For now, I concentrated on watching Puck come apart from having that tail inserted in his pert little bottom by his pragmatic trainer. I had no doubts that Kamal would give this young gentleman whatever he needed in the way of strict discipline, punishments and even rewards. If anyone could whip a ponyboy into shape, it seemed to be *this* man, whose presence demanded deference.

I almost pitied the kid, who didn't look more than twenty-two or twenty-three. But when he locked eyes with me and licked his bottom lip in a deliberate way, jiggling the silver ring that pierced his tender flesh, I wondered if that ponytail wasn't exactly what Puck wanted. And being taken in hand by a trainer like Kamal, and humiliated in front of the ranch boss and the new photographer?

When Kamal was done, he took hold of Puck's harness and pulled him to a stand. The young man groaned and fixed me with long-suffering, blown pupils, and a look that almost brought me to my knees.

"Thank the nice gentleman, Puck. And apologize."

Puck licked his lips again, closed his eyes and mumbled, "Thank you, Oliver. I'm sorry for how I behaved earlier."

I tried to reply but nothing came from my throat. My name, spoken from the mouth of this sexy boy who had come here to play pony and now might be regretting it, or *not regretting it at all*, had jolted me to the core. I wanted to hear him say my name over, and over, and I wanted it to mean something more than it did right now.

"You're welcome, Puck," I finally managed, in a voice rough with unexpected emotion.

His eyes snapped open and he lifted his chin to give me a sharp, assessing gaze. We held each other for a long moment, at which point the corner of his lip twitched. Then Kamal pulled him away from me, buckled his armbands together, and shoved him toward the fence.

"Trot. Three times around the paddock. Go."

My breathing had ramped up with the excitement of the encounter, and I cleared my throat, glancing at Adam who watched with understanding and amusement.

Kamal grinned. "Don't get too attached to that one. He may not last."

My eyes widened. "Do you lose some of them?"

I'd only just met Puck. I didn't want him to leave the ranch right when I'd arrived.

"Not often," Adam said. "Usually, we see if they do better with another trainer first."

Kamal raised an eyebrow. "You want to try him with Lorraine?"

Adam thought for a moment. "Not yet. Let's see how he is after this session. If you didn't break him with that, there's hope he's doing all right. I'm not sure what's going on with him. I offered to speak to him as a counsellor, but he wasn't interested."

Kamal nodded. "I feel like there's something else going on. He's having a difficult time focusing."

Adam crossed his arms on the fence and watched Puck trot, to the best of his ability, around the ring as I returned to his side.

"So, Oliver, do you think you'll be able to adequately represent the spirit of ponyboys like Puck in your images?" he asked.

"I sure hope so," I said, gaze captured by the strength and grace of Puck's movements, and the sight of the thick, black horsehair tail swishing across the backs of his legs.

Adam and Kamal chuckled.

"Come on, Oliver. I want to show you the bunkhouse," Adam said.

We walked along the dirt trail that led from the grooming barn, past the arena, to a smaller wooden building on the edge of the trees.

"This is where the ponyboys stay while they're here. The male stable hands bunk here as well. They help keep the ponyboys in line in the bunkhouse, and it's good for them to be able to bond with each other, since they come into intimate contact in the grooming barn."

My brain spun with this information as Adam opened the bunkhouse door and we stepped inside.

"Liv stays at the main building, simply because she wouldn't enjoy being housed with this rabble, and it keeps things copacetic. Lorraine is at the main house as well, but that's because she's a trainer and they're all housed there."

"I see," I said, gaze flying around the space, landing on the confused features of three men—two relaxing on wooden bunks and the third, grabbing something in the kitchenette at the back.

I was still reeling with my paddock encounter, and the bunkhouse seemed astonishingly ordinary.

"Gentlemen, this is Oliver, our visiting photographer," Adam announced. "Oliver, this is Lincoln, Teagan, and...Joshua, right?" he said, gesturing to each of them.

The tall man in the kitchen nodded and moved toward us. "That's me. Hi, Oliver."

"Hello. Glad to meet all of you."

Joshua had a hipster look to him, with long hair in a bun, a short beard, and an eyebrow piercing. Teagan was blond and bulky, with thick muscles and a square face. Lincoln had the same lean, almost skinny physique as Andrew, but with brown hair rather than red. They were attractive men, and if I wasn't on a pony play ranch, and hadn't just seen Puck, at least one or two of them would have turned my head.

As it was, I still had the image of Puck in mind, and probably wouldn't get rid of it for a while.

"How are you finding things so far?" Adam asked, leaning against the bunk where Teagan sprawled with a gaming magazine open on his lap.

"Stellar," Joshua grinned, peeling the wrapper from a granola bar and taking a bite, watching me with interest.

"You have a great set-up here, Adam," Lincoln said. He was small with light-brown hair and a sweep of freckles over his nose and cheeks. "This would be a great spot for a summer festival or something like that."

Adam laughed.

Teagan nodded. "Yeah, like Coachella, but for kinky people."

"Great idea," I said because it was, and I could picture it.

I turned to Adam. "I have to say, I'm impressed. The setting is fantastic and the variety of locations for shooting is wonderful. I love the authenticity of the environment. I'm sure I can produce some spectacular images for you."

"Glad to hear it." He clapped a hand on my shoulder. "Look, we should get back to the main house. I have work to do, and you can have a rest or go exploring on your own. Supper is out back of the main house at around five thirty. All the staff and ponyboys convene for a cookout. Unless it's pouring, in which case we gather in the cafeteria."

I smiled at the three men in the bunkhouse. "I'll see you later."

I noticed Joshua giving me a look-over and winking to Teagan, who shook his head, but I pretended I didn't.

On the walk back to the main house, Adam said, "I noticed you had a connection with Puck this afternoon." He eyed me. "Or am I mistaken?"

I was suddenly conflicted. Should I deny it, and say I was overwhelmed by everything? Or should I tell the truth? I felt like Adam would know if I lied.

I glanced at him and nodded. "Yeah. Maybe. Seemed like it."

"Looked like it," Adam said.

"Is that against the rules?" I asked curiously, after a little while.

Adam laughed. "No. Not for you. Or Puck."

His answer made me feel relieved and anxious at the same time.

"But be careful, will you? Something's going on with that one, and he won't tell me what."

I nodded. "Okay. Thanks for the heads-up, Adam."

He put a friendly hand on my back as we ascended the porch steps. "Of course. I'm looking forward to what you're going to produce while you're here, Oliver."

I held the door open for him.

"Now that I've observed the ranch in operation, Adam, so am I."

CHAPTER FOUR

THE EARLY MORNING DEW

OR

FIRST ASSIGNMENT IN THE GROOMING BARN

I DECIDED, AT the risk of appearing stand-offish, that I'd skip the communal supper. I checked with Adam, who said it was fine, since I'd met everyone of consequence already. But he hoped I'd avail myself of the experience most days, since my meals were included with my stay.

I honestly wasn't that hungry. I was more excited than

anything else. I had been prepared for the gear and the submission, and even for Kamal's expert domination skills, though the entire enterprise was eminently impressive.

But I hadn't been prepared for the raw sexuality and appeal of Puck in the paddock, bent over with his hands clutching the rough wood fence, while a butt plug horsetail was inserted unceremoniously into his rear.

I'd anticipated being blown away with it all. And I had been.

I was so impressed by the ranch and so excited about taking photos of these beautiful creatures for six weeks, I wanted to chart out the way I would approach my assignment and figure out a plan.

I'd start in the grooming barn tomorrow, because that was where the experience began for the ponyboys. In the afternoon, I'd get some shots of the ponyboys with their trainers. Maybe later, I'd take candids in the bunkhouse and the main house. None of these images would include faces or other identifying features.

I could hardly wait to get started.

*

IN THE MORNING, I rose early, showered, and dressed in

tan cotton shorts and a blue short-sleeved button-down. I pulled on my white chucks, which I'd never be able to wear on an actual horse ranch, but they seemed perfect for a day at the BCR—comfortable and hip. I desperately wanted these cute ponyboys to think I was hot. Yes, my mind was on obtaining professional and artistic images of all the dirty details, but I wanted to present an alluring image myself.

Especially when it came to Puck.

I ran into Kamal on the main floor, a cup of coffee in his hand as he made his way along the hall.

"Good morning, Oliver."

"Good morning, Kamal."

"There's fresh coffee in the cafeteria," he said, with a smile. "And you'll find cereal in the cupboards, and fruit and milk in the fridge. Help yourself."

"Thank you."

"I'll be in the front room if you'd like to join me?" he pointed a bit further down the hall.

"Sure. Thanks."

I grabbed a banana and a cup of coffee and found the room Kamal had spoken of. It was actually at the back of the main house—or the front, I suppose, depending on your perspective—with large windows and comfortable furniture arranged in a pleasing way. Kamal was seated in an armchair by the window, sipping his coffee and making notes on a piece of paper which he folded and put in his pocket when I approached.

"Looks like it's going to be a beautiful day," he said cheerfully, tossing his pen onto the wood and black-metal coffee table.

"Yes."

I stood at the expansive windows, sipping my coffee and staring out at the green fields and paddocks. The sun glinted off the walls of the grooming barn and arena, and the bunkhouse was a small brown dot in the distance.

"I take it you're a city boy?"

I smiled. "Yep. Don't get out to the wilderness very often."

"Hmm. I hope you don't find this place boring. There's not much to do but enjoy the beauty of nature and play with kinky young men."

He winked.

I laughed.

"Mm hmm. I figure my work and the...scenery...will keep me entertained."

"What did you think of my contrary ponyboy?" His deep

brown eyes pierced me with curiosity.

I shrugged. "You mean Puck?"

"Of course, I mean Puck."

I laughed and scratched my chin. "Hey, I'm new here. I don't know how many cranky ones there are."

"Fair enough." Kamal smiled.

"He seemed...pissed off about something. Do you get a lot of ponyboys like that?"

"No, not really. Most of them are quite happy to be here, kinking it up, and it's more of an intense game than anything else."

"Sure."

"Then again, it's not uncommon for this type of role-play to trigger deeper, unaddressed issues in some men. They think they want to play pony, but they aren't prepared for the immersive nature of the ranch. Or the demands of trainers like myself."

"I imagine. You seem very...dedicated."

Kamal chuckled.

"That's one way of putting it. The ponyboys I train might use a different word."

I laughed. "Sure. But I bet they like it. For the most part."

He grinned and sipped his coffee.

I peeled my banana and took a bite, staring out at the sunlit grounds.

*

I DECIDED TO grab my camera and stroll the fields in the early morning, before the trainers and ponyboys began their official duties, to capture the beauty and innocence of the area.

There was dew on the grass and birdsong pervading the cool air, and the heat from the rising sun forecast a steamy day ahead. I spent some time taking shots of the grooming barn and arena from the outside.

Then I walked the dirt track to the bunkhouse and took some shots of it too, wondering what was going on inside those wood walls. At the moment, I was far enough away to not be invading anyone's privacy. But I hoped to eventually take some non-identifying photos of the men inside, those willing to share their daily lives with me.

First, I'd have to get to know them.

I aimed my Nikon at the edge of the forest, where squirrels and chipmunks frolicked and antagonized each other, and birds landed on branches to observe the cresting dawn, when the creak of rusty hinges made me glance at the bunkhouse.

A young man emerged into the morning light, and it only took me a second to recognize the dark-haired man I'd seen in the paddock with Kamal the day before.

Puck.

He took in my presence with a disdainful glare and walked forward, stopping before me with his arms crossed over his chest.

"What are you doing here?" he asked. He was wearing faded jeans with a rip in one knee and a LEGO Star Wars T-shirt, which I couldn't help finding completely adorable.

I straightened from my crouch and smiled.

"Good morning."

"Is it? Yesterday you watched that prick give me my tail, and today you're creeping around taking pictures of the bunk-house. You realize we don't play pony in there, right?"

Jesus, he was a spitfire. Despite our chemical attraction in the paddock, it seemed I'd gotten on his bad side.

"I know. I was only taking shots of the building."

Puck assessed me, and I think if it hadn't been strictly forbidden on ranch property, he'd have pulled out a pack of cigarettes and smoked one. He looked me over slowly, not saying a word, his expression stony as I stood there. I tried to think of something else to say since he wasn't exactly rushing to fill the silence.

"It's a beautiful morning" was all I came up with.

Puck didn't take his eyes off me as he responded. "I guess. I shouldn't be up this fucking early."

"Oh?"

"I don't have to be in the grooming barn until one," Puck said, scratching beside his freckled nose and yawning. "I should have slept in."

"Why didn't you?" I asked, trying not to be seduced by this man's arresting physical form which seemed to belie his ornery soul. But he was fucking sweet-looking, with his soft black hair that curled at the edges in the summer heat, and his delicate, freckled nose, lean stature, and full mouth. The jewelry in his eyebrow and lower lip glinted in the sunlight.

He didn't answer right away. Then, miracle of miracles, the hint of a grin and the words, "Really? If you don't think putting nine guys together in a communal space is going to make for noisy sleeping arrangements, then you're dumber than I thought."

I held onto that grin like a lifeline and ignored the derogatory comment.

"Good point," I said. "Well, since you are up, and I've

got my camera, would you allow me a few shots?"

He narrowed his eyes. "I don't want to be identified."

"Of course," I nodded. "I only want you from the neck down."

It took a second for both of us to register what I'd said. Puck smiled slowly, and I felt the heat rise in my cheeks as I scrambled to dissemble. I cleared my throat.

"I mean, I'll only photograph you from behind or from the neck down. That's all I meant."

He regarded me curiously, and again I saw an invisible cigarette dangle from his lips. He was that cool. He radiated it. Although, I had the feeling it was an intentional deflection from more unstable emotions.

"Are you sure?" he asked. There was no teasing this time. It seemed like a sincere inquiry, and I struggled to answer it with the same honesty.

"No," I said, "But as far as my photographic license goes, I'm not allowed to take a photo of your face." I hesitated, looking at the ground, then glancing back up. "As much as I'd maybe like to."

We gazed at each other for several moments. Then he shrugged.

"Whatever. Do what you want. I need to take a piss. You

can shoot that if you want."

"Um... Isn't there a bathroom inside?"

Puck laughed, turning only slightly to the side as he un-zipped his fly and dug his cock out of his pants. "It's crowded right now with the morning crew. I thought it would be more private out here." He held my gaze as a jet of bright yellow piss arched out and landed in the grass, steam rising from the shock of heat on the cold morning dew.

I don't know what possessed me, but I had promised to capture life at the BCR, and Puck had given me permission. So I lifted my camera and took a few shots of Puck emptying his bladder onto the ground, as my heart beat hard in my chest.

"Wow," he said when he'd finished. "You're dedicated."

"Yeah, well, you're gorgeous. Even while pissing onto the ground with a crappy attitude." I grinned at him in order to temper my words. It was all so true.

He stared at me—I think surprised by my forthright com-pliment.

"Hmm," was all he gave me by way of a reply as he tucked himself in and zipped his jeans. He turned away and stepped up to the bunkhouse door, and I figured that was it. But he turned back as he grabbed the handle.

"The crappy attitude comes and goes, and the rest is just good genes. How old are you, anyway?"

My mouth went dry as I melted under the fire of his gaze. "Just turned thirty. You?"

He looked me over. "Not *that* old." He opened the door and went inside, where I heard the sounds of other men speaking and laughing before the door shut behind him.

Fuck. He'd known right where to hurt me. Whether he'd intended to or not, I didn't know. Anyway, I was older than he was, obviously. Maybe too old to be interesting. We'd have to see, then.

I may not have been old enough to be real Daddy material, but I was old enough to know this boy, perhaps, needed a Daddy more than anything else right now. As much as he tried to play it cool, he seemed lost and out of his depth—fragmented and trying to reassemble his identity in this unusual setting. I wanted to comfort and guide him, even though I had no idea if he'd want me to. In fact, after our interaction just now, I knew I'd have to play the long game with him. I'd need to convince him I could be good for him, because he seemed skeptical, at the very least. And I had no doubt there were a few others who were going to make a play for Puck.

But I had six weeks. I was better at marathons than

sprints anyway.

*

I WALKED BACK toward the grooming barn and tried the staff entrance. It was unlocked, so I stepped inside and found Lorraine, the female trainer, writing on the whiteboard with a fat marker.

She smiled at me. "Good morning, Oliver."

"Good morning," I said. "Do you mind if I get a shot or two of your hands as you write? Since I'm here. It's Lorraine, right?"

"Yes. And, no, I don't mind at all."

She continued to write on the whiteboard as I moved in close beside her so I could shoot over her shoulder.

The camera clicked as I took several angles of Lorraine's delicate fingers on the marker, writing *basic gear* under the name *Joshua.*

Andrew, Puck, and Justin had been in training yesterday afternoon, which meant Joshua, Teagan, and Lincoln were on this morning. The three attractive men I'd met in the bunkhouse would be naked and washed and tacked in front of me this morning.

Lorraine put her marker in the tray and turned to me. "I

see you are going to be recording every last detail, Oliver."

I grinned. "That's my job. Adam wants a record of everyday life on the ranch. So, not always the sexy shots of bare asses and harnesses."

I recalled shooting Puck's early morning piss in the dew. Whether that would make it into the official collection, I had no idea. But something told me Adam would appreciate the raw and natural beauty of the moment.

Lorraine nodded and leaned seductively against the rectangular table, which held harnesses and efficiently arranged supplies. She looked me over carefully, then folded her arms across her chest.

"What's your story, Oliver?"

I felt put on the spot. "Pardon?"

She smiled, flashing her teeth.

"What made you say yes to the opportunity to document the daily life at this kinky place? Hmm? Pure monetary motivation? Curiosity? What?"

It was a fair question.

"Well, to be honest, I needed something to fill my summer. So there was definitely a monetary component behind it. This is how I make a living."

"Fair."

"Curiosity? Definitely. How does a place like this exist? How does it run? What do the ponyboys look like in person? How is a ponyboy trained?"

"So many questions," she said dreamily. "Have you gotten any answers?"

"Starting to. But this place is so detailed—so immersive—it's probably going to take me the full six weeks to figure it out."

Not to mention it was going to take the full six weeks to prove to a certain ornery ponyboy that I could show him a few things he might enjoy—and hopefully get him to fall for me during the process.

"Well, you'd better get started, then," Lorraine said, walking past me to the door and glancing back. "I'm looking forward to seeing what you produce."

She flashed me a smile and was gone.

I set my camera bag down and unzipped it, before pulling out the tripod. Once that was unfolded and situated, I pulled out my Canon EOS R5 and attached the zoom lens, then slotted it onto the tripod. I had taken my older Nikon camera on walkabout earlier, and it did a fine job, but for more steady work I liked the pricey Canon model.

The door opened behind me, and I turned to see Liv and

a man I hadn't met yet enter the grooming barn.

"Hi, Liv. I hope I'm okay to set up in here?" I asked.

"Hey! Yeah, sure. As long as you stay back from the shower area and right beside the table, it should be fine."

"I might want to come in for some closer shots, but I'll use my handheld camera for that. I'll try not to disrupt you too much."

She smiled. "Adam wants us to accommodate you to the best of our ability. So don't worry. We'll let you know pretty quick if we need you to get out of the way."

I laughed. "Perfect."

"This is Adrian, by the way. He's on the morning shift with me this week."

"Adrian," I said, by way of greeting.

"Oliver." He looked me up and down and gave me a quick smile. "You sure you're up to taking close-ups of sweaty muscles and leaking cocks?"

I blushed. "Um...I'm sure I will be up to it. I've done fetish photography before."

"Ah. An experienced player. I like it."

"I've photographed some stuff. Nothing quite comparable to this though," I admitted. "This animal role-play business is new to me."

I heard the other door to the building creak open, and footsteps sound behind the partition.

"Ponyboys are here. Better get set up," Adrian said.

I hastened to make some final adjustments to the camera as Liv and Adrian sorted items on the table. I saw the flash of silver and heard the thud of leather, while voices in the other room gradually quieted and the first naked man rounded the corner.

Teagan, without his clothes on, was a blond God.

Thick muscles in his legs and arms, a six-pack that looked like I could bounce a ball off it, and a dick the size of a prize cucumber made my eyes bug out of my head. But I schooled myself quickly, in order not to appear like an absolute newb. I'd seen a hot naked guy before. Even with his seemingly physical perfection, Teagan's nude presence didn't touch me the way Puck's ethereal beauty had.

I started shooting as he moved to stand beneath the showerhead closest to the left, and Adrian slid in beside him, a black ball gag in his hand. With deft fingers Adrian placed the gag between Teagan's pliant lips and fastened it behind his head.

"Arms up."

Teagan raised his arms and glanced at me with curiosity.

I almost lifted my hand in silent greeting, but these men were supposed to be animals or objects once they had entered the grooming space, so I didn't acknowledge him—just kept taking photos of his body with the zoom lens, following as his wrists were buckled into the hanging cuffs and Lincoln came around the corner.

Lincoln was cute, with a smaller cock than Teagan had, but with a streamlined body that would look good on a fashion runway. Adrian quickly gagged Lincoln and attached his wrists to the hanging cuffs above his showerhead and then moved to the table to grab a loofa, as Liv went to deal with Joshua.

Joshua was boy-next-door attractive and imperfect, like Puck, in a way that made my juices flow. His hair was down now and fell past his shoulders in soft brown waves. I wasn't particularly a fan of long hair, but Joshua pulled it off. His body was thicker than Lincoln's but not as built as Teagan's. There was a certain innocence in him that appealed to me. He probably wasn't naive at all, since he was playing pony on a fetish ranch, but he had the look about him. As Liv placed the ball gag between his teeth, I caught a flash of something far from innocent in the gaze he shot me.

After the gags and wrist cuffs, the cock cages came out. I'd seen these before, but never in use.

Liv must have seen me staring, because she grabbed something off the table and tossed it in my direction.

"Here. Have a closer look."

I caught and examined the contraption in my hands. It was made of stainless steel and consisted of a large ring that I expected fit around the base of the ponyboy's penis and balls, and then several smaller rings on a central bar that curved along a four-inch span. I imagine they came in different sizes.

"This is, well, it's nice." I hefted the metal device in my hand, enjoying the weight of it.

"Nice?" Adrian said, with a chuckle.

I shrugged and gave the device back to Liv.

The stable hands tucked the ponyboys' penises into their assigned cock cages. It made sense to do this before things got out of hand and the ponyboys became so aroused it made the task impossible. As it was, Adrian struggled with Teagan's massive appendage but managed to fit it into the largest device.

As the consummate professional I professed to be, I zoomed in on this procedure, because it seemed so important to the overall hierarchy of the ponyboys at the BCR as lowly servants and obedient animals. They would presumably be reliant on their trainers for any relief from the confines of these strict restraints.

It would be interesting to see which of these men photographed well, and which didn't. The camera could be fickle, although usually that was more apparent in portraits. I would be capturing body parts primarily, and more would depend on the angle of a particular shot and the lighting, than on the charisma of the model.

At least, that was the theory.

I took a collection of long shots as the ponyboys were rubbed and scrubbed to cleanliness as my practical mind appreciated the thoroughness of the stable hands and marvelled at the way the men were treated like animals to be groomed and prepared for their trainers. It was a wonderful way to get them into the service headspace needed for their sessions.

"Is it all right if I come in closer, Adrian?"

"Sure," he said, giving me a glance.

He glided a wet cloth over Teagan's captive privates as the large ponyboy closed his eyes and widened his legs to allow the stable hand ample access.

I crouched and took shot after shot of Adrian's skilled fingers as he cleaned Teagan, front and back, then got several different angles of the ponyboy's plump buttocks and solid legs.

Then I moved on to Lincoln, who waited patiently for one of the stable hands to be done with the others and attend to him. He watched me out of curious eyes, saliva beginning to slide down his chin from the gag. Seeing these men like this was a trip–more so than anything I'd experienced at other fetish shoots. There was an authenticity about it. It wasn't simply people playing dress-up and experimenting with a casual power exchange.

I was the recipient of many curious glances from the ponyboys and even the stable hands, since it was my first morning, and they hadn't yet gotten used to my presence. I hoped to become a part of the landscape eventually, so that I could effectively record what went on at the ranch without becoming a part of it. I was paid to be an observer. I truly wanted to be a fly on the wall when I was behind my camera.

When I wasn't behind my camera, I'd continue to try to blend in so I'd get an honest idea of the workings of this unique place. I planned to keep a diary of my experiences, so besides the photos, I'd have a personal record of this very unique opportunity.

If I could record, in words and images, even a half of what I'd seen and felt so far, I'd be richer for it.

CHAPTER FIVE

LORRAINE AND TEAGAN

OR

AN EARLY MORNING REWARD

I CALLED MY first morning in the grooming barn a success.

When the stable hands took the ponyboys to their trainers, I scrolled through the images I'd taken, and my belly
clenched with excitement—both at the raw sexuality and
beauty captured in the shots and at the photos themselves.

I was pleased. This project beat taking photos of fruits

and vegetables in so many ways. I wasn't sure I could go back to that, to be honest. But I wasn't going to worry about it right now. I couldn't fight the silly grin on my face as I folded up the tripod and packed my fancy camera into its bag.

Liv and Adrian returned shortly.

"Hey, Oliver," Adrian said. "Did you get some sexy shots?"

"Oh, yeah."

"Lorraine wanted me to suggest you take some photos of her session with Teagan, if you want to," Liv said as she got to work tidying up. "They're in the arena right now."

Hmm. I'd already packed my fancy gear away, but I had my handheld.

"Sure. Is it okay if I leave my gear here? I'll just take my small camera." I held up my compact Nikon.

"Yeah, of course. Just tuck it beside the table. It'll be safe."

I nodded. "All right. Have a good morning, then."

Adrian smiled, waggling his eyebrows. "You too."

I grinned. "Plan to."

I exited the grooming barn and came to a stop, overwhelmed again by the majesty of the setting.

Green and gold grass stretched to the edges of the thick

forest on three sides and to the main house and parking lot on the fourth. Adam had mentioned a spot on the lake for swimming, and I looked forward to taking advantage of that very soon. The day was already hot.

I gazed at the bunkhouse in the distance, wondering if Puck had returned to bed or if he was up and wandering around, or reading a book, or playing video games. The image of him from that morning came back to me, causing my mouth to dry and my cock to thicken.

I stopped and scrolled through the photos on the Nikon to the ones I'd taken of Puck pissing into the morning dew. When I saw them, I returned to that raw and intimate moment, experiencing again Puck's disdainful attitude and my helplessness to do anything about the attraction I felt.

The photos were stunning. There was something about Puck that had captured me and that my camera had picked up. Even taking a piss in the early dawn, the lines of his body seemed otherworldly.

Then there was the quick close-up I'd taken with the zoom.

In a way, taking pictures of cucumbers and zucchinis had been good practice for framing shots of penises. I examined what I could see of Puck's uncircumcised dick as he performed the most basic of acts. It was a medium-sized, ordinary dick in its relaxed state, but I couldn't help admiring its soft curves and the way the foreskin hugged the head as the yellow piss streamed forth.

I'd captured the action, so to speak, and there was no doubt what was going on. The long shots of his stance, open jeans, hand holding onto himself, and the hot piss arching into the dewy grass were surprisingly erotic, if someone was into men. Maybe even if they weren't.

I took one last look at Puck's casual stance and clicked the viewer closed, walking forward and pulling open the door to the arena. As soon as I stepped inside, the thump of boots on floorboards echoed and Lorraine's voice sounded.

"Knees up. Good. One more circle of the room and then come stand for me."

I closed the door and walked to where Lorraine stood in the middle of the room, watching Teagan as he trotted at a moderate pace. Although I was incredibly attracted to Puck's lithe form, I appreciated the sight of Teagan's substantial muscles and tight glutes, emphasized by the leather harness and posture-enhancing armbands.

Where Puck was a fiery colt, Teagan was a prize stallion—the epitome of commercial male beauty in a kinky, equine package—beautiful and strong and majestic. While his presence didn't affect my heart and soul the way Puck's did, my cock hardened and my heartbeat quickened at the look of him.

I lifted my camera and took a series of quick, offhand captures as he jogged to us and Lorraine greeted me.

"Oliver. So glad you could join us."

She didn't take her eyes off her charge but watched him closely as he slowed and stopped in front of her.

"Thanks for the invite."

"Of course. You might as well see what you'll be working with." She reached out and lifted her hand before Teagan's face, presenting the back of it to him. "Lick."

Obediently, Teagan's lips opened and his pink tongue emerged to swipe across Lorraine's brown skin as she smiled.

"Very good ponyboy. You have pleased me."

At her words, Teagan stood taller and glowed with pleasure. His cheeks, flushed from the exertion, darkened further as he waited for instruction.

"Oliver has come to take some photos of you, Teagan."

The ponyboy's gaze shifted to me with suspicion and, perhaps, jealousy? He'd seemed curious about me and my camera in the grooming barn, but now I sensed a protective energy from him, as if he didn't want to share his mistress with anyone.

I couldn't blame him, really.

Lorraine, although tiny, had the gravitas of a much larger person. She had a masculine energy, clothed in a feminine package. I sensed an indomitable will.

In a different but equally valid way to Kamal, she commanded respect.

Charisma? Presence?

Whatever it was oozed from her pores like a truth serum.

"Answer me," she said in a deceptively mild tone.

"Yes, Ma'am."

"Will you stand still and let Oliver take some photos?"

"Yes, Ma'am."

Teagan's blue eyes shifted to me as he extended his neck and lifted his chin.

"He's covered with sweat and breathing hard, Oliver. Take some photos before he cools down. Show what a pony-boy's body looks like after a good trot around the arena."

"Sure," I said.

I had been tempted to say "Yes, Ma'am" but managed to stop myself.

I lifted the camera and circled Teagan, taking shots of his

backside, thick thighs, and strong calves. The Docs on his feet were scuffed with use and I imagined each pair was worn by a multitude of different ponyboys. I focused in on the boots' utilitarian and much-fetishized appeal as Teagan stood motionless before Lorraine.

Then I took shots of Teagan's broad back, dotted with beads of perspiration, and his powerful shoulders and neck. I came around in front of him and captured the swell of his pecs and abdomen framed by the leather straps of the black body harness. A sweep of blond hair covered Teagan's chest and a narrower trail led under the pelvic strap of the harness to where his huge cock nestled in its steel confines like a sleeping tiger.

"We had to find the extra-large cage for this one," Lorraine murmured, reaching out a delicate finger to touch one of the metal bars of the device, close to Teagan's bulging flesh.

He hissed quietly and visibly resisted moving away from her touch.

"We have the applicants send in their measurements when they register, so we can plan out some gear, and when we got Teagan's we double-checked that they were accurate, then found the extra-large cage from our very first session. We had a ponyboy named Henry that first session who needed a big cage, but we haven't used it since. He was a gorgeous red-head. Well, he had red hair in other places too." She winked.

Teagan shifted his feet as Lorraine continued to touch the bars of the cock cage, occasionally gliding her pretty finger over Teagan's swollen flesh with deliberate intent.

"They like to be teased, Oliver. Most of them. They like being trapped with no hope of an orgasm until their trainer takes the damn thing off."

"Do they?" I asked, unabashedly taking close-ups of the delicate curve of Lorraine's forearm, her small brown hand, and the slim finger tracing designs on Teagan's captive cock. Nobody seeing these photos would know the subjects by name, only as *ponyboy* and *trainer*, but the dynamic would be obvious.

"Yes, they do. Teagan knows he is mine to do with as I please during his training session. And he only hopes that he pleases me enough by being obedient, following my instructions, and excelling at the tasks I set him, so I uncage him and give him some relief at the end of it."

I stopped shooting for several moments as the meaning behind this statement of Lorraine's sank in. I lowered the camera and met her frank gaze.

"You mean, you—what do you mean, exactly?"

She smiled with an honest pleasure as she said, "If a ponyboy is good for me, I uncage him and jerk him off at the end of the session. It's a reward for good behaviour and a motivation for the same."

I blinked, picturing this confident and intimidating woman unlatching Teagan's cage and taking him in hand to the point of orgasm. My cock, which had exhibited a relatively casual interest in the proceedings so far, perked up with interest.

I cleared my throat and adjusted myself. "Really?"

She nodded. "Really. I glove up, of course. Wouldn't want to get any fluids on me. We do take certain precautions here at the ranch, even though everyone is screened."

The way in which she spoke of this—*procedure*—made me thrill to see it. But I didn't have time to stay for Teagan's entire session this morning. I'd promised Adam I'd take some still shots of the main house before joining him for lunch. Lorraine must have seen the disappointment on my face.

"What's wrong?"

"I just—" I laughed, embarrassed. "That sounds like quite the thing. But I have to get back to the main house, and I won't be able to stay for Teagan's session in order to—see how things–come off."

Lorraine laughed. "What a shame. Well, he has been astonishingly pliant for me already this morning. I could demonstrate right now."

Teagan made an eager noise as his eyes flew wide. A shudder wracked his body as Lorraine jiggled his cock in the device, as if guessing at the weight of bagged produce.

I puffed an excited breath out. "Okay. Sure. Yeah. I'd like to see that."

"Hmm, what do you think, Teagan? Can I count on you to continue with the good behaviour for the remainder of your session if I reward you now? Sometimes it's more difficult to give your all after you've climaxed. You'll have to fight against the natural urge to lie down."

"Yes, Ma'am. I'll be good. I promise." Teagan's voice was deep and husky, full of desire for what his trainer had proposed.

Lorraine smiled and shrugged, looking at me. "Some of the ponyboys are reluctant to have a female trainer. They don't think I can match a man for dominance and skill. They soon learn that I can."

She lifted her forearm in the air, straightening her fingers and pressing her thumb flat against them, so her hand became a streamlined triangle. She swivelled it slowly to emphasize the delicate shape and winked at me.

"Small hands can be an asset. They can get into all kinds of secret places." She gazed meaningfully at Teagan's ass as he paled and uttered a gasp. The thought of petite, delicate Lorraine burying her small hand and forearm in Teagan's ass made my cock throb. Teagan shuddered.

"You know, we do keep very long gloves at the ranch, for special occasions."

"Good Lord," I commented, blushing.

"You seem to be taking all of this in stride, Oliver. Do you have experience with heavy kink?"

I inclined my head. "I've been involved in some fetish photography in the past, yes. But not to this level. It's been an education."

She giggled. "Oh, you will learn all kinds of wonderful things during your stay, I'm sure."

Lorraine deftly unlatched the cage surrounding Teagan's penis. As she slipped it off, his cock swelled and straightened in front of us. The girth of it was intimidating.

"You'd think I'd need both hands to tame this monster," she commented. "But I've found if I use one hand in just the right way, it works fairly well."

Teagan groaned and licked his lips, glancing from

Lorraine to me and back to Lorraine. He shifted his feet as his cock swayed and leaked before him.

"Here, Oliver," Lorraine said, wrapping the empty cock cage in a handkerchief she pulled from her pocket, then passing it to me. "Put it on the table and come back here."

"Sure," I said, tearing my eyes off Teagan's erection and doing Lorraine's bidding.

By the time I returned to them, Lorraine had pulled on a nytril glove and was squeezing lube out of a small tube into her hand, while Teagan watched with eager eyes.

"Spread your legs, Teagan."

Teagan moved his legs apart and Lorraine wrapped her small hand around his large appendage and began to work it.

I lifted my camera.

Teagan's gaze shifted to me as he made soft noises of pleasure. I wished I could capture that look on his face, of rapture and pride and gratitude. His cheeks were flushed from exertion and arousal...and perhaps some embarrassment at being on display. But I aimed the camera lower and focused on Lorraine's hand and Teagan's cock as things got going.

She was right about her technique. Lorraine was clearly adept at handling penises. Her fingers seemed to be everywhere at once. She changed up her tempo and her grip to keep him engaged, and the fact that his arms were captive and he was under the curious gaze of a virtual stranger must have made the situation that much more effective.

My brain and body responded to the tantalizing image of the muscular ponyboy at his trainer's mercy, his dick an entertaining object in her expert grasp. Lorraine's petite lips opened as she concentrated, and Teagan's moans of bliss became stuttering gasps as he approached his climax.

With a series of practiced twists of her delicate wrist, Lorraine brought Teagan to the edge and over it, the milky surge of his semen oozing over her knuckles as she continued her manipulations. Teagan's primal groan echoed off the walls of the arena, and I took a series of photo bursts of the event as my heart hammered in my chest and my cock throbbed with envy.

When Teagan's orgasm waned and he sagged with relief, Lorraine released him and peeled off her rubber glove, crooning and reassuring her charge.

"Very, very good. I think Oliver got some lovely photographs of you, my pet."

I cleared my throat, attempting to quell my own excitement. "I did. Lots."

"Hmm. I think Oliver appreciated our performance in more than simply an artistic capacity."

I glanced down at my shorts where a definable tent from my erection was visible. I shrugged and grinned.

"Can you blame me?"

I wasn't embarrassed in the least. What gay man wouldn't have gotten hard from that?

The tinkling of Lorraine's musical laugh soothed my spirit and revived my energy. I began to take shots of her ponyboy's penis as it slowly softened and shrank. I zoomed in on a bubble of semen as it emerged from the tip of Teagan's cock and hung, suspended by an extending thread, before separating and dropping to the floor.

That image would make it onto the website. I was almost positive.

"Lorraine. Teagan. That was incredible. Thank you." I replaced the lens cap and smiled.

Teagan said nothing, but Lorraine touched my arm. "You're very welcome, Oliver. Come back and watch us anytime you like."

She left Teagan to recover and took her soiled glove to the wastebasket under the table. I followed, knowing I had to get back to the main house but not wanting to leave.

She glanced at me. "Are you interested in watching Kamal with Puck this afternoon?"

Oh, dear God. Yes, yes, and yes.

"Sure," I said, pretending to be blasé about it.

"I'll let him know to expect you, then."

"Thank you."

"No, thank *you*, Oliver. I can see that Adam has hired a consummate professional. I have no doubt you will do the BCR proud with your captures."

"I certainly hope so."

I walked back to the main house, leaving Lorraine and her spent ponyboy to the remainder of their session. Teagan would have to reassemble his energy. It would be a slog but he might just be hard again by the end of it. Perhaps, if he was a very good ponyboy, Lorraine would reward him a second time.

My mind returned to the memories of her long fingers working Teagan over, and I tried not to get hard again. But the anticipation of being in the ring with Kamal and Puck this afternoon made me giddy with desire.

CHAPTER SIX

A MOMENT OF OPPORTUNITY

OR

HOW TO GENTLE A NERVOUS PONY

ADAM AND I met for a sandwich in the cafeteria.

"I promise to take you for a proper lunch on the weekend. We'll go to the resort café. I want to show you the fancier side of the BCR's business model. And, of course, you'll have a prime spot for the pony show on Saturday.

I grinned. "Can't wait."

"Did you get to catch a training session this morning?"

I nodded. "Yes. Lorraine and Teagan"

"Lorraine was a wonderful find. Kamal suggested her, I interviewed her, and by the time I got to see her in action, I had no doubt she'd fit in here."

"Were you hesitant to hire a woman? Because you deal with ponyboys?"

Adam shook his head. "No, not really. Most people involved in extreme kink respect a person in a position of authority over them, regardless if it's a woman or a man. They get off on the power and the dynamic. The gender of the person wielding that power is often irrelevant."

"Have you ever had trouble persuading a ponyboy that a female trainer would work for them?"

"Sometimes they're a little disappointed to find out they haven't been placed with an alpha male trainer. They soon discover that Lorraine has her own particular brand of discipline and control."

"Yes, I can see that," I said, recalling what I had seen that morning.

"She's one in a million and I'm keeping her."

I raised my glass of water. "Hear, hear."

When we'd finished eating, Adam stood.

"I must get back to my office. Lots of paperwork to take care of when a new session begins."

I stood as well and shook his hand. "Thanks for bringing me in. I can already tell this is going to be an incredible assignment."

"I can already tell you're going to be up to the challenge, Oliver."

I glanced at my watch. According to what I'd been told, the afternoon ponyboys would be arriving at the grooming barn right about now. I was sorely tempted to shoot the second set of young men in the showers and getting tacked but decided to go to my room instead for a short rest. I'd be shooting Puck and Kamal in the arena or the paddock, and I wanted to preserve my artistic energy for that.

Upstairs, I unplugged my phone from its charger and sent a text to Grif to see if he was available for a phone call. It didn't take him long to answer.

YES. Just let me close my door. I'm at the office.

Grif worked as a financial consultant at CIBC. Kind of the farthest thing from what I did, but maybe that was why our friendship worked so well. Plus, I had access to free investment advice.

He sent me a thumbs up emoji a moment later, and I hit the Call button. He didn't even let it ring fully before he answered.

"Ollie! Hi! Oh my God, how is it? Have you ridden a ponyboy yet? Gotten one to eat sugar out of your hand? Tell me!"

I broke out laughing. "Uh, no. I don't think they actually put saddles on the ponyboys here. Or ride them."

"Oh. That's kind of a bummer."

"If you say so. And the one ponyboy I'd love to feed sugar cubes to would probably spit in my face if I tried."

Grif inhaled a sharp breath. "Ooh! Tell me more!"

"The ranch is fantastic. It's huge and there are—"

"No, no. Go back to the ponyboy that would spit in your face."

"Grif—"

"What's his name? I mean his real name, not his pony name. Oh, wait, what's his pony name? Is it Lightning?"

I sat down on the loveseat and rested my forehead in my hand.

"You're too much."

"I'm not the one at a ponyplay fetish ranch who wants to talk about the landscape, my friend."

"Fine," I said, hesitating for a moment before I continued. "His name is Puck."

"That's his pony name."

"No, that's his real name." I blinked. "Well, I don't know if it's his real name, but it's the name he's using while he's here. It's not his pony name."

"Cool. What's his pony name?"

"I don't know! Jesus, would you let me talk?"

"Sorry. I'm sorry. I just spent the morning going over financial forecasts with four different clients. Can we please talk about sexy ponyboys?"

"If you shut up, we can."

"Fine. Zipping it. Go on."

"Thank you. So, his name is Puck, and I swear he is the sexiest motherfucking thing on two legs at this place." I grinned, now recalling Kamal's authority and stature. "Although, his trainer, Kamal, is damn hot also."

Another loud inhale. "*Kamal.* Oh my."

"And knows just how to get Puck to behave himself. Which seems like a pretty big ask, actually."

"Oh, good Lord. A *naughty* ponyboy? I'm feeling faint. Good thing I'm sitting down."

"Anyway," I said, not wanting to talk about Puck anymore

because I didn't want to jinx things. Not that there was anything to jinx. But, still. "I spent the morning in the grooming barn."

There was a pause. "The, what now?"

I cleared my throat. "The grooming barn."

Another pause. "What the fuck is a grooming barn? And, are you serious?"

I laughed. "Yes, I'm serious. It's a barn where the guys are showered, rubbed all over with a loofa, their cocks put in cages, while they're bound by their wrists to an overhead rail."

Grif didn't say anything, but I heard the creak of his desk chair. "What. *What.*"

"Mm hmm. It's something to see. Oh, and then they get tacked into their harnesses and collars, and sometimes they get bridles and butt plug horsetails, but I haven't seen that yet."

Oh, wait a second. Yes, I did see that.

But I wasn't going to tell Grif about Puck in the paddock the day before or he'd probably mess his pants.

He sounded breathless when he replied.

"Oh Lord, Ollie. You're killing me here. My pants are a little tight."

"No doubt. Anyway, I got some great photos."

"*Anyway, I got some great photos,*" he imitated me in a sardonic tone. "Bastard."

"Oh, come on. Can't you be happy for me?"

"No. Yes. I don't know."

"Uh-huh."

"Suddenly, my life seems so very boring and conservative. I need to up my game." There was a pause. "Where do they find their trainers?"

"Not at CIBC."

"Fuck you."

I laughed. "Fuck you too. Anyway, I've got to go. I'm shooting Puck's training session this afternoon, and I want to chill for a bit first. It's been a busy day."

"Mm hmm. You mean you want to enjoy a quick wank."

"That's not a bad idea."

"I wish I could do the same. I officially hate you, by the way. Keep me updated. *Please,* keep me updated."

"Sure. Bye."

We ended the call and I got a glass of water and made sure I had some lube before I sat on the edge of the bed and took myself in hand, recalling the things I'd witnessed that morning and yesterday. It didn't take long, and I was glad to take the edge off before lying down and trying to read a chapter of the book I'd brought with me.

But I couldn't concentrate and gave up after ten minutes.

*

THE WEATHER WAS cooler today. In fact, I had found the outdoors a little chilly that morning, so I grabbed an orange and black plaid button-down and threw it on over my black tank top leaving it unbuttoned. I'd forgotten to wear my baseball cap earlier, but put it on now, in case Kamal had Puck in the paddock again.

As I approached the arena, I noticed two figures in the nearby corral. When I got close, my heart rate sped up as I realized who they were.

Kamal. And Puck.

They were in the far corner. Kamal stood behind the young ponyboy, who was tacked in the standard gear–body harness, armbands, collar, cage, and boots.

No tail yet, which, to be honest, was a bit of a disappointment.

Kamal leaned close, his hand wrapped around Puck's wrist, next to the armband which fastened to the one on Puck's other forearm. He was speaking to Puck, who nodded occasionally and concentrated, his brow furrowed.

I kept my distance as they seemed to be enjoying a private moment. I chose a spot by the nearest fence and busied myself setting up my tripod and camera, which only took a few moments.

When I glanced up, they were in the same position, but Puck's wide-eyed gaze was on me as he listened to Kamal.

When my gaze met his, the electric shock of cellular-level recognition hit me like a Mack truck. We barely knew each other, but there was a biological pull between us. That was for damn sure. Chemistry, attraction, allure, animal magnetism—whatever it was left no room for denial. I hadn't felt anything close to this in years. My hookups had been random and quick, with people I was attracted to, in theory. But not with this level of instant combustion. They had been convenient, more than destined.

I was under no illusions that this was anything more than a situational obsession and would likely dissipate once we got to know each other a bit more, since that was always the way of things. I had already put him on a kinky pedestal, as my ideal sort-of cantankerous brat-boy in kinky pony play accessories. But I might as well enjoy it while it lasted.

My dick, which had become interested upon my spotting of the mostly naked ponyboy, now went full bore at the same time my gut churned with agitation. The potent current be-tween us attracted Kamal's attention, as Puck's chest rose and fell more quickly, and he shifted his feet nervously.

Kamal looked up and followed Puck's side-eyed gaze to me. The intimidating trainer narrowed his eyes but nodded and lifted a hand in acknowledgement of my presence.

I gave him a salute and returned my gaze to Puck's. He had turned his head now to watch me. But Kamal said some-thing else that made him wrench his gaze from mine and glare straight ahead, nodding in acquiescence.

Puck seemed determined to behave himself this after-noon and I wasn't about to disrupt that honourable intention. I'd remain as inconspicuous as possible in order to get the shots I needed, even though my body and mind thrilled to see him so effectively chastened by the older man.

The kink scene had always been a source of fascination, and I'd encountered enough men who wanted to play casually at power dynamics, but I'd never really taken it seriously. Def-initely not as seriously as the Braided Crop Ranch did. I'd done some bottoming in my twinky twenties, but even when I had, I'd preferred being in control of everything. Once I'd gotten braver and more able to state my preferences to the men who seduced me, or whom I seduced, I'd discovered the joys of topping. I considered myself a switch, but I liked to be in control.

So as I watched Kamal step back and give Puck a hearty slap to the backside, which propelled the ponyboy into a jerky trot, I felt an equal desire to fuck, and to be fucked, by this beautiful creature.

I didn't care one way or the other. I'd take what he had to offer.

Now that I was here, at the Braided Crop Ranch, in this heady environment where domination and submission was the *entire point*, I couldn't help a gut-wrenching need to explore the dynamic in ways I never had before.

Over the next thirty minutes, I watched Kamal put Puck through his paces, and took a slew of photos of them working together. Puck seemed determined to perform to Kamal's satisfaction, and though there were occasional glimpses of the contrary attitude I'd witnessed previously, he tamped it down and gave it his all.

Kamal was clearly pleased with him, and when they finished an extensive lesson on form and comportment, the trainer brought Puck closer to where I stood, presumably so I could get some closer shots and hear the praise he doled out.

"Very good, Puck. You've done incredibly well, and I'm happy to reward you for your hard work."

My gaze flew to find Puck's. We locked onto each other as Kamal's fingers deftly unlatched the cage around the pony-boy's swollen tackle.

This felt different than watching Lorraine and Teagan. Because Puck was my obsession, and so far, I'd only seen him prance around in his pony gear and piss into the grass.

Now, as Kamal freed his cock, Puck kept his gaze on me and lifted his chin as if to say, "Yeah, you want me? Can't have me right now, but you can watch me get jerked off into the dirt."

Fuck.

My shorts tightened as Kamal pulled a nytril glove from the pocket of his jeans and pulled it on, then added lube from a pump bottle near the fence. As he rubbed the slick substance on his fingers, he glanced at me and grinned.

I started to feel lightheaded and wondered if I should leave. Was I ready for this?

"Aren't you going to take some photos, Oliver? I thought that's what you came for."

Ah, fuck.

I was standing there beside my expensive photographic

gear, staring wide-eyed at Puck, completely oblivious to the purpose at hand.

"Oh. Yes. Of course. Yes. Sorry."

I cleared my throat and fumbled in my bag for my handheld, feeling like I should move closer but terrified Kamal would notice how this was affecting me. Maybe that ship had sailed.

By the time I'd got sorted out and approached them, Kamal had moved in behind Puck and slung a powerful arm across the ponyboy's chest, keeping him steady, as he lazily jerked his cock with his gloved hand. Puck's head lay on Kamal's shoulder, his eyes shut and his lips slightly parted, as if he'd completely given up fighting the man and decided to willingly surrender to his dominance.

At least for today.

"Jesus," I muttered under my breath as I raised my camera to get the shots I needed–close-ups of Kamal's thick bicep against Puck's heaving chest, the ponyboy's bare legs framed by Kamal's clothed ones, and Puck's bare ass pressed against Kamal's clothed groin. The juxtaposition of their bodies was beautiful and almost poetic.

The noises that came from Puck's throat sent tremors through me as my dick ached and heart pounded. And

Kamal's hushed commentary was just as arousing.

"Good boy. That's it. Relax, I'm not going to hurt you. I just want to make you feel good."

Puck whimpered as I took photo bursts of Kamal's skilled hand job. When he groaned with sudden volume, I made the mistake of glancing up to find his dark gaze on me, as Kamal kept his movements slow and steady. The trainer wasn't making this quick but extending the ponyboy's pleasure at the same time as he made him wait for release.

My mouth dry, I held Puck's gaze for several moments, then turned back to the viewer. I wanted to capture the moment of release when it happened. The money shot, so to speak.

My heart beat fast and sweat gathered on my neck, but it was too late to take off the plaid shirt. I swallowed thickly as I crouched on one knee with my camera aimed at the action.

Puck began to squirm as he got closer to his orgasm, trying to push his cock into Kamal's tight fist at the rhythm he craved. But Kamal held him still and continued his slow, steady tease. Puck whimpered and gasped, his struggles becoming more desperate. Kamal's arm strained to keep him still and the older man's lips pressed together with determination as he murmured soft reassurances into Puck's ear.

Finally, when I thought the poor kid would scream from frustration, Puck stiffened and a stuttering wail erupted from his throat, as semen gushed over Kamal's moving hand.

"Good boy. That's a good boy, so very good, Puck."

If I'd been closer to Puck's age, I probably would have creamed my jeans at the sight of this. Instead, I used the monumental will I'd gained from so many years of practice and locked my desire down, continuing to take photos as Puck sagged against his trainer and shuddered through the remnants of his orgasm.

But my breathing laboured, and my heart beat with abandon.

Kamal held him until Puck regained his energy and stood stiffly, cheeks flaming with embarrassment as he tried to avoid my gaze.

Kamal peeled off his soiled glove.

"Oliver, I'm going inside for a second. Can you keep an eye on him? I'm sure he won't be any trouble," Kamal said.

"Uh, sure. I'll stay right here," I said, watching Kamal walk past and out the gate.

Acting on sudden impulse, I lifted the camera and took a burst of shots of Kamal from behind as he strode toward the arena with the messy glove clutched in one hand.

As I lowered my camera, I watched Kamal for a few more seconds before turning to meet Puck's challenging gaze. He stood there, spent and satisfied, with a scowl on his face and lines of concern marring the skin of his forehead. He was still the most beautiful thing on two legs.

I shrugged and smiled. "He's hot."

But nothing compared to you.

Puck's eyes narrowed and he snorted, sounding like a real pony.

"If you like bossy assholes who use their power against you," he muttered.

His comment sounded ridiculous in the circumstances, and I couldn't help laughing.

"What did you think you were gonna get at a pony play ranch? Some pushover?"

He nodded, cheeks darkening. "Fine. Yeah, sure. Laugh at me. I know you think I'm ridiculous."

That sobered me.

"Puck. What?"

He squirmed, like he wanted to leave but knew he had to wait here for Kamal, and if he didn't, he'd be in some major trouble that he probably didn't want to think about.

"I mean, what kind of guy would want to do this, right?"

he said, gazing at the paddock around him as if it were full of refuse.

"You're seriously asking me that?"

He glared at me.

I continued. "I think there are a lot of men who would want to be standing in your shoes." My gaze drifted along his body to his scuffed Docs. "Boots," I corrected. I gestured around us at the ranch. "Clearly."

He didn't say anything, but his gaze very deliberately roamed over my body and back to my eyes. "Would *you?*"

I felt my cheeks heat. *Would I?*

I didn't know what to say, so I took off my baseball cap and slapped it against my thigh. The sound made Puck jump. Which was more telling than anything I'd seen so far.

He covered his startle with a sneer, though, and repeated his question.

"Would you?"

"Sure."

"Yeah, right."

I stared at him, wondering how long Kamal was going to be. I felt abandoned and put on the spot. But maybe I should take advantage of the privacy we had.

"I'd be open to trying it," I said.

"Awesome. Next time I see Adam, I'll let him know that our expert photographer wants to try life as a ponyboy."

"I'd rather be a trainer," I said, glancing to see if Kamal was making his way back yet. There was no sign of him, so I turned back to Puck.

He watched me, his eyes bright with interest. I moved carefully, cautiously, closer, as if he were a wild horse and not a human ponyboy on his way to being domesticated.

He held my gaze as I neared. I stopped in front of him.

"*Your* trainer," I said, raising my hand. I held it in the air near his face, waiting for a sneer or a curse or even a wad of angry spit.

He glanced at it, then returned his gaze to mine as I lowered it so my fingers landed on his hair. I stroked my fingers over his dark locks as he closed his eyes and sighed, like the weight of a thousand burdens had been removed.

"I think you're beautiful," I said, savouring his perfect bone structure and pale skin spattered with beauty marks.

He said nothing as he stood beneath my touch. He kept his eyes closed, but his chest rose and fell with quickening breaths.

I leaned in and placed a soft, chaste kiss beside his nose. He turned his face enough to press his cheek against my lips and expose his neck, as if asking for more, when a throat cleared nearby.

We jerked apart.

I stepped back and gazed apologetically at Kamal. "Sorry. I'm sorry."

Kamal's expression was one of pleased surprise. He only shook his head.

"It's quite all right. I told you to watch him. I just didn't think you'd watch him quite *that* closely."

"I'm sorry," I said again. "I couldn't help it."

Kamal grinned and gestured to Puck who stared at the ground and scowled.

"I completely understand. For such a contrary ponyboy, he's incredibly appealing."

Puck snorted and scuffed at the dirt with his boot.

"Good luck," Kamal said, then laughed and raised his eyebrows, shaking his head at me.

"Thanks," I muttered, retreating to pack my gear.

I was officially done for the day. I needed to get some space, reassemble my thoughts and emotions, and decide what the hell I was going to do now.

CHAPTER SEVEN

INTO THE WOODS

OR

NOT A VERY SMOOTH SEDUCTION

I GAZED AT the crowd on the front lawn of the main house before descending from the porch and stepping onto the grass of the lawn. Adam waved me over to where he stood beside Kamal at the large grill, conversing in the evening light.

I walked over, scanning the group of gathered people but not seeing the one man I was actually looking for.

"Oliver! Glad you made it down for supper today," Adam said. He held a *Mad Tom IPA* from the Muskoka Brewing Company in his hand and took a swig while Kamal flipped a burger on the grill.

"You are multitalented, Kamal," I said, grinning.

Kamal winked. "I don't just jerk off ponyboys, you know."

God, I felt like I'd known these people for weeks already, and I'd only been on the ranch a couple of days. Someone bumped my elbow and I gazed down into Liv's smiling face.

"Howdy, Oliver. Want a beer?" She held an IPA out to me.

"Sure. Thanks," I said, taking it and tipping it to my lips. The cold amber liquid quenched the edges of my thirst.

"How's the photography going? Think you've got enough subject matter to keep you busy for a while?"

I laughed, waggling my eyebrows. "Oh yeah. I've only tapped the surface of this place."

"But what a surface!"

Adam spoke up. "I can attest that the money we're paying Mr. Lambert is well worth what we're getting."

I'd forwarded Adam a few of the initial shots, and he'd seemed very happy with them. Beforehand, I had gone over all the captures, and I was excited to select the very best, make minor adjustments, and pretty them up with filters. But I'd kept the images as raw as possible to maintain the authenticity of the ranch and give viewers the feeling they were seeing something real.

"Thank you," I said, tipping my beer in his direction like a salute.

"My ponyboy seemed to enjoy your visit to the paddock," Kamal said, turning hot dogs with a pair of tongs.

I frowned. "Really? He looked like he wanted to drive a stake through my heart."

Except for at the end, when Kamal had left us alone and Puck had pressed his cheek against my lips when I'd kissed him. Or had I only imagined it?

Kamal rolled his eyes. "Some of these ponyboys speak a different 'love language,' that's all."

I blushed. "Oh," I said, while Adam chuckled.

"'Love language' or 'sex slang'? Maybe 'sex slang' is a better term, Kamal," Adam said.

"Yeah. Anyway, I think he likes you, Oliver." He waved his tongs at me and smirked.

"Well, I...don't know what to say about that."

Adam put a hand on my back. "Just remember what I

said."

He exchanged a glance with Kamal, who rolled his eyes.

I nodded. "Sure."

I cleared my throat and redirected the conversation away from me.

"Don't you have kitchen staff?" I asked, gesturing around at the cafeteria workers who were bringing out bags of buns and paper plates.

"Yes, but some of us *like* to grill," Kamal said, "After a day of wrangling recalcitrant ponyboys, I like to handle *easier* meat."

Liv howled with laughter while Adam chuckled.

"Nice," I said.

Kamal held his free hand up for a high five, and I delivered it.

Lorraine joined us, a beer in hand and Teagan at her elbow. The young man looked good in his denim shorts and short-sleeved button-down and followed Lorraine like an eager puppy. He glanced at us, but his gaze returned to Lorraine as if he didn't want to be distracted.

"You just like meat, Kamal. Any meat," Lorraine commented in her silky voice as she lifted the bottle to her smiling lips.

"Guilty."

We chatted good-naturedly until supper was laid out on the buffet table.

As I was squirting ketchup onto my burger, someone bumped my elbow.

A good Canadian, I immediately said "Sorry" and moved, even as my ketchup landed on the edge of my bun and dripped onto the plate.

"You overshot."

I turned my head to see Puck standing right beside me.

He looked delicious as usual, wearing jeans with holes in the knees, pink Docs, and a blue Twenty-One Pilots T-shirt. My heart started going a mile-a-minute as he reached out a finger to scoop some of the red condiment from my plate and then met my gaze as he sucked the digit into his mouth.

Sudden heat rose in my face as we regarded each other. I managed to scrape out "That was your fault" as my body went onto high alert.

He grinned and winked, as his tongue emerged and slid across his bottom lip, over the silver ring there. "Not the first time."

Now I was standing in front of the buffet table with an erection, as more people gathered to load up and grab napkins and utensils.

Puck chuckled and moved along to load his plate, leaving me wondering what to do. I took some of the potato salad, feeling awkward and blindsided. I wanted to leave the ball in his court. I wasn't going to follow him around like a love-struck teenager, even if that was how I was starting to feel.

I needed to chill. My mind was spinning. Puck had actually approached me. And had—*flirted* with me?

Adam waved me over to his table, and I headed there, where Liv, Adrian, Kamal, and Lorraine had joined him as well.

"You must be hungry," Lorraine said, gesturing at my plate which I'd filled with samplings from most of the food on offer. It was the first substantial meal I'd eaten at the ranch, since I'd been so busy and preoccupied.

"Starved. I've been on the go since early this morning," I said, glancing around and finding a familiar pair of eyes on me again.

Puck sat with three other ponyboys, but he stared at me. When I met his gaze, he narrowed his eyes but held mine, while I recalled our chance meeting at the bunkhouse that morning with a full body thrill.

"You must have a lot of pictures by now," Liv

commented. "I'm hyped to see some."

I nodded, tearing my gaze from Puck and smiling at Liv. "Good."

"I imagine we should have some sort of a slide show once the session is nearing its end," Adam suggested.

"Adam, I can't wait that long," Lorraine whined.

"I suppose it might motivate the ponyboys to perform if we show them some of the images sooner than that," Adam agreed.

"Good idea," Kamal murmured, observing me closely. He must have caught Puck watching me.

I engaged in pleasant conversation with my tablemates and was grateful for such a comfortable welcome to what was probably the kinkiest fetish ranch this side of the American border.

I glanced up to look for Puck every now and then, but he seemed to have disappeared. I tried to concentrate on the topics of conversation at the table and enjoy the delicious meal.

Eventually, supper was cleared away and various dessert options, as well as carafes of coffee and tea, were placed on the buffet table.

"You'd better get dessert if you want any, Oliver," Lorraine suggested. "It tends to disappear rather quickly."

"Good idea," I said, standing and taking my dinner plate to the recycle bin. I grabbed a dessert plate and approached the rectangular table. As I reached for a fudge brownie, a hand slipped in front of mine and grabbed the one I'd been going for.

My gaze tracked Puck's slim fingers as they lifted the brownie to his parted lips and pushed it inside. He chewed, with a slow grin, watching me as he devoured the dessert with astonishing efficiency. Transfixed by the motions of his jaw and throat, I barely noticed as he reached for another, larger square and dumped it onto my plate. He leaned close and said, "You want something even tastier in your mouth? Meet me at the bunkhouse tomorrow morning, seven sharp."

I blinked as the blood in my body headed immediately downwards. "Okay."

Puck cocked his head. "You better be there. If I get up that early for nothing—"

"I'll be there."

He saluted me and then he was gone, striding over to the group of ponyboys gathered several metres away.

I stared after him, but he didn't make eye contact again. He joined in their conversation and effectively ignored me. I grabbed another brownie off the serving platter and added it to my plate—if I wasn't going to have my carnal hunger quenched until morning, I needed more chocolate.

*

I FELL ASLEEP as soon as my head hit the pillow but woke only a few hours later and tossed and turned for the rest of the night. Images of Puck in the paddock and how he had looked first thing in the morning, sleep-tousled and soft-eyed, appeared whenever I closed my eyes. I gave up at five and got up to shower and then went downstairs for something to do.

The main floor of the house was quiet, so I used the kettle in the cafeteria to make a cup of instant coffee and took it, and a breakfast bar and banana, into the front room. I stood at the expansive window gazing at the BCR grounds as the sky lightened, enjoying the peace and quiet as I swallowed my emergency caffeine. I planned to enjoy a cup of the better stuff once the staff had made it for the morning meal.

Seven o'clock seemed an eternity from the present moment and by six thirty I had become so agitated I couldn't keep still. I worried that someone would come downstairs and I'd have to explain why I was getting such an early start. With my Nikon strapped around my neck, I could use the old photography excuse, but I imagined I might nevertheless look suspicious, especially if Puck's subtle stalking of me at supper the previous evening had been noticed.

I managed to wait until six forty-five before heading out.

The ranch was so tranquil at this time of day. It soothed my soul if not my agitated heart and body. I didn't know what to expect from my meet-up with Puck, although he had alluded to something *tasty*. I couldn't dwell on what that could possibly mean, or I'd combust from excitement.

I'd dressed in a pair of faded denim shorts, Bermuda-length with frayed edges, my white chucks, and a worn Bowie T-shirt.

The bunkhouse sat quiet at the edge of the trees, although I could hear the muffled sounds of movement from inside when I got close. The morning shift of ponyboys would be preparing to head to the grooming barn.

There was no sign of him, so I wandered around photographing the grasses, trees and foraging wildlife while I waited and my gut swirled with anticipation. I only hoped he remembered our plan, or that it hadn't all been a silly prank.

A latch clicked, bringing me out of my head. I lowered my camera and turned to see Puck slip out the door, raising his hand to shield his eyes from the bright morning light.

Thank God.

"Good morning, Sunshine," I said, throwing him a relieved smile.

He grunted and yawned, then jerked his head in the direction of the trees. "Come on."

I lifted the camera from my neck and followed him, gaze drifting over his slender form in faded skinny jeans rolled at the hem, slip-on purple Vans and a bubble-gum pink T-shirt. He looked fucking delectable. He checked behind him to make sure I was following and looked me over, giving me a one-sided grin before facing forward again without another word.

"Where are we going?" I asked, keeping the volume of my voice low in the hushed dawn although there wasn't anyone else around.

"Into the woods, and through the trees."

I recognized the quote from the Disney musical, even though he hadn't sung it. If he had, I would have had confirmation he was a magical sprite come to tempt me.

"All right?" he asked, angling sideways and extending his hand without slowing down.

"Yeah."

I laced my fingers in his, and he pulled me along, until we were winding through the forest on a narrow, leaf-covered path that was barely there.

I had expected him to be grumpy since that's pretty much how he had interacted with me so far. Which didn't bother me. He could be irritated with me as long as, deep down, he wanted me with him.

Maybe he knew by now I was on his side.

Once we'd reached the thick of the forest, Puck dipped under the branches of an oak tree, grabbed my T-shirt in his fist and pulled me so hard my body slammed against his. Our faces were inches apart. He held my gaze with an intensity that almost vibrated the slight bit of air between us as his chest moved up and down, his breaths matching my own.

"Fuck, I need you to kiss me," he said, that torrid gaze burning into me and setting my heart aflame.

I didn't answer, instead taking a moment to hang my camera on its strap over a nearby branch. Then I brought my hand up to cup his chin and angle his face as I took his mouth with mine.

Puck groaned and tilted his head, opening up to me. We were all testing lips and tentative tongues for a moment until he grabbed the back of my head and pulled me in.

I caged his body against the tree trunk and rubbed up against him, feeling his arousal and pressing mine into him.

He grunted and hissed like a wild thing, holding me tight and letting me plunder his mouth. His frantic heat enveloped me as we rode a current of mutual desire.

He tasted of fresh mint and smelled like sun-warmed bedsheets, and I inhaled him like a fine vintage, grabbing at his mouth with mine and shoving my tongue inside. He panted and groaned like he wanted me just as much, and I could barely believe it. His grip on my shirt tightened as he held me against him. I could have stayed there for hours.

We had to come up for air. While we caught our breath, I peppered his chin and throat with tiny kisses. I'm not sure how many times he said my name before I heard him over the pounding of my heart.

"Oliver..."

"God...what?"

"I need you."

"I need you too. What do you want?"

He pulled my face down to his again and kissed me, slower this time, with a grin. "I brought lube."

Oh, Jesus. He wanted—*that?* Here? In the woods?

I stopped kissing him and pulled back to gaze down at his hooded, sex-starved gaze.

"Jesus. I don't have a condom."

"I brought that too."

I stared at him, my dick throbbing but my brain hesitating. "Wait. Really?"

"Yeah."

I gazed around us at the trees and the rough ground. The cool breeze did little to quench the fire inside me, but I felt cautious.

"Well...we just...I mean..." I stalled. My trembling fingers strayed to the front of his jeans almost of their own volition.

"You don't want to?" he asked, nipping at my chin and darting his tongue out to lick, while he thrust himself against my hand.

"Of course, I do. But maybe not yet. How about I suck you off instead?"

"Not yet?" he said in a small voice, as if he were worried that I didn't want to fuck right away. But he recovered quickly. "You like making me wait?"

"Sure. Yeah."

He chuckled softly. "You think the payoff will be worth it?"

I grinned. "I know it will."

"Fine," he sighed, hands going to his waistband.

"Or," I said, "Maybe I should get a blow job. Since you

dragged me all the way out here, away from my comfy bed at the main house."

Seeing that shred of vulnerability, when I'd felt like I was on the back foot with him, made me bold. As I suggested this turning of the tables, I nuzzled his ear and rubbed my knuckles against his hardness to win him over.

He closed his eyes. "Princess."

I pressed my mouth to his ear and breathed, "Ponyboy."

Puck stuttered a sigh, then dropped to his knees, and before I knew it, he had my shorts open and was pulling my cock out of my briefs. I braced my arms against the tree trunk as he wrapped his fingers around me.

"You don't waste time." I said, then gasped as he engulfed the head of my dick in his warm mouth, gaze on mine. He sucked hard, making me whimper, then pulled off and stared at me, moistening his pretty lips with his tongue and nudging the steel ring.

"We have less than six weeks to figure this out. We don't have any time *to* waste."

He batted a nosy fly away and bent to my cock again, swirling his tongue around the head and then plunging down, making me curse.

"Fuck! Okay. So, not just a one-time thing?" *Thank God!*

His answer was to take me deeper and tug my shorts down so he could cup my balls in his hand and press a finger against my taint.

"Oh, fuck," I cursed, lust swirling deep inside like a tsunami. "Jesus!"

He pulled his mouth off again and narrowed his eyes. "You want to come in my mouth?"

My chin dropped slackly. "Please."

He smirked. "So polite. Say it."

"Say what?"

"Say you want to come in my mouth."

Puck tightened his fingers and licked his tongue flat across my glans, making my knees want to buckle. That tree trunk was the only thing keeping me upright.

"I want to come in your mouth," I said.

Unfortunately, while inhaling sharply at the sound of those words in the innocent forest air, a mosquito or large gnat flew into my throat and was vacuumed into my windpipe.

I froze, choking, then coughed several times and spat to the side, trying to get whatever it was out of me.

Puck slid his mouth off me and stared.

I waved at the air. "Bug! Bug down my throat. Fuck. Sorry."

I continued to cough and spit into the grass, finally able to dislodge whatever it was. I gasped air into my desperate lungs while Puck observed me with a wry expression.

"Holy shit. If that's how you react with a tiny little bug in your throat, Oliver, I guess it's good that I'll be showing off *my* blow job skills today."

I cleared my throat and spat once more, to make sure the stupid insect was gone. But I nodded in acknowledgement of his comment.

"Yeah, laugh it up," I said while he snorted into the back of his hand, trying to hide his smile. "I'd rather choke on your cock over a bug any day."

He gazed up at me with amused eyes and smiled. "Glad we're on the same page, then." He gave me a full-on smile before bending to my dick again.

I braced my arm on the tree and threaded my fingers through his soft hair, closing my eyes and warning all unwelcome insects to fuck off while I enjoyed this welcome little interlude.

All thoughts of invading insects left me as I thrust into the delicious heat of his mouth and closed my fist in those dark locks.

The vibrations of Puck's low groan reverberated through

my cock.

I was already fucking close, despite the bug debacle, and I think he knew it. But the tables were turning. With my fist in his hair I held his head still and fucked into his mouth, meeting his gaze to make sure he was still on board.

He opened his jaw as wide as he could, gazing up at me with a calculated doe-eyed look that almost put me over the edge. He unzipped the fly of his jeans and slipped his hand inside them, grabbing his cock and pulling on it while I used him. He breathed rapidly through his nose and stroked himself, while my rhythm automatically ramped up and I pumped hard into his warm throat.

Puck's eyelids fluttered closed as his face flushed and beads of sweat appeared on his forehead. He released his hold on my dick and grabbed onto my thigh with one hand as if he needed to keep steady while I used him. He grunted and choked, his other hand working faster where it disappeared into his jeans.

Finally, he stiffened and made the most vulnerable sound as his hand slowed, then jerked hard twice and he was coming, his face a paroxysm of pleasure and relief.

When I realized he'd just come in his pants, I cursed and stilled, the orgasm barreling through me like a herd of wild stallions trying to reach a mare. His eyes opened and bugged as my jizz pushed out between his lips, too much for him to deal with. He sputtered and groaned with frustration, trying to swallow and pulling off to lick me all over while I rode the aftershocks and gaped down at him.

Jesus fucking Christ.

The world stilled around us. Birds chirped and cicadas hummed as we collected ourselves.

Puck leaned forward and rested his head on my thigh where his hand still clutched me.

"Holy. Fuck."

He coughed and wiped his other hand across his mouth. It might have been my imagination, but I think his fingers trembled.

"You okay?" I said, attempting to help him to his feet when my thighs were still quaking.

"Sure. My undies are messed though." He laughed, as he stood and swayed.

"Careful," I said, clutching his T-shirt and pulling him in.

He crashed against me and we canted into the tree trunk. I kept us upright somehow and laughed, grabbing his narrow hips and bending to peer at him. He was frowning down at himself, wiping ineffectually at the mess he'd made.

"Puck," I said gently.

He glanced at me from beneath his lashes, so shy and calm and different from the kid I'd seen in the paddock with Kamal. He was...vulnerable and open and my heart just about died.

"Was that too rough?" I asked, pressing my forehead against his.

He smiled, then frowned, then smiled again. "No. I liked it. I came in my fucking pants, didn't I?"

I circled a hand under his chin and tipped his face to mine. "Yeah, you did. So damn hot." I traced his chin with my finger. "Are you a dirty little boy?"

His breath caught, and I saw a flash of renewed desire. "Fuck," he breathed. "You have no idea."

I pulled myself together, fixing my shorts and tucking myself away. Puck fastened his jeans over his soiled briefs. Then we rested against the tree, sharing soft, quiet kisses in the peaceful forest, satisfying a mutual need to touch and be near each other.

I fingered the steel over his lower lip. "I love this, by the way. It feels so good when you kiss me."

"I got that in high school. Wanted to look cool." He shrugged.

"What about the eyebrow one?"

"Couple of years ago. A friend dared me."

"I like it too," I admitted.

"You got any?"

"You would have seen them by now, I think. Nope."

He regarded me seriously.

"I haven't even started to see you, Oliver Lambert." His eyes raked over me like he wanted to remember the way I looked right this moment. "We'd better get back."

"Hold on. Speaking of names. Is Puck your real name or an alias you're using?"

He threw his head back and laughed. "It's real. My mom teaches high school English."

I grinned. "That is awesome. Because I like it very much."

"I'm just glad it wasn't Prospero. *The Tempest* is her other favourite play."

"Fuck, you'd make any name sexy as fuck."

He raised his eyebrows. "I don't know about that."

We stood silently regarding each other. He glanced in the direction we'd come.

"You go first, and I'll wait for a bit, so nobody sees us together," he said.

"We're keeping this quiet."

"For now…"

He blew a soft breath against my face and gave me a quick kiss before pulling away and turning into the trees. He lifted a hand to wave. He looked so beautiful—a picture of light and shadow with the morning sun slanting through the leaves.

"Wait a second," I said, grabbing my Nikon off the branch and removing the lens cap. "May I?"

Puck shrugged, looping his thumbs in his pockets and glancing down at his crotch. "Can you tell I came in my pants?"

"It hasn't soaked through your jeans. Yet."

"Then hurry up. I gotta get back before it does. It's cold and sticky."

"Stay still then. Look pretty." I said, framing him from the waist up and clicking several times.

"Always," he said, then stuck out his tongue and flipped the bird.

I laughed and took the shot, then lowered the camera. "These are for me. I won't show them to anyone."

"Good."

"Thanks for the blow job," I said.

"Thanks for a healthy breakfast." He grinned, tongue

snaking over the ring in his lip.

"Hmm. I don't think you got enough. I'll have to feed you again."

"Can't wait," he said, and then he was gone, turning and jogging through the trees.

And I was standing in the middle of a forest in the Muskokas, wondering why the world looked different all of a sudden.

I walked a bit further on the path to take some photos of a fallen tree and some interesting fungus before making my way back to the open field beside the bunkhouse. When I emerged from the trees I saw Andrew and Joshua standing by the door, speaking together in hushed tones.

"Hey," I said. "Good morning."

"Morning," Joshua said. "You're up early."

I nodded, attempting to look like all I'd been doing was taking wholesome pictures of birds and squirrels and not fucking Puck's face in the woods. I'm not sure I pulled it off. Something told me the fact I'd just spent twenty minutes getting my rocks off with the BCR's cutest ponyboy was written all over my face.

"Yeah, it's peaceful in there." I waved my hand at the trees and the calm fields. "Y'know. Nature and all that."

"Uh-huh. Nature," Andrew said.

He had his arms folded across his chest and was grinning like he didn't believe a word of it. They must have seen Puck come back to the bunkhouse from the same direction. They weren't stupid.

I didn't linger. I lifted my camera and gestured toward the main house. "Anyway, gotta get back and have another cup of coffee."

Joshua eyed me suspiciously. "You gonna take pictures in the grooming barn?"

"After lunch," I said. "The afternoon crew."

"Ah. That'll be us," Andrew said, smiling.

"I might pop into a training session this morning. Not sure yet." I said, heading toward the main house.

"Okay. See ya maybe," Joshua said, giving me a salute.

I inclined my head and faced forward, trying not to swagger as I made my way along the path.

Kamal was standing on the porch, leaning on the railing with a coffee in his hand. He examined me as I approached, like he knew exactly what I'd been up to.

"Oliver. You're up early."

I blushed, feeling guilty about lying to Kamal. But that didn't stop me. "Yeah, well, the fields and the forest are quiet in the early morning. Nice ambience."

Kamal grinned. "If you say so."

"I'm gonna get some coffee," I said, climbing the stairs and moving past him as he chuckled.

I decided to go back to bed to recover from the morning's exertions and my disrupted sleep. I set an alarm for eleven so I'd be up in time to get some lunch and be in the grooming barn when the afternoon ponyboys arrived.

CHAPTER EIGHT

VOYEURISTIC INTENTIONS

OR

PRELUDE TO AN UNAVOIDABLE RECKONING

I DREAMED OF a giant gnat choking me on its huge, human cock.

When I woke, I was very hard and extremely confused, until I recalled inhaling a bug in the woods while my dick was in Puck's willing throat.

Puck...

My hand drifted to my erection and I teased myself, re-membering the way his pretty lips had felt around me. The sensation of the steel ring had added to an all-around stellar experience. Even the humiliation of the cock-blocking insect inhale didn't matter in the long run.

And *now*...now, I was going to have a quick lunch and head to the grooming barn with my equipment, so I had an excuse—a very good one—to watch Puck and his two ponyboy shiftmates, buffed and caged and shined in preparation for their afternoon training sessions.

Watching the grooming procedures yesterday had been eye-opening. Seeing the object of my intensifying obsession being carefully and tenderly prepared for training would be something else entirely.

I happened to pass Kamal on my way downstairs.

"Are you in the grooming barn this afternoon?" he asked.

"Yeah, I'm just getting something to eat. I'll head over there soon."

He smiled. "Good. Planning a special treat for you. I hope your camera battery is charged."

Oh my fuck.

He chuckled as he went on his way.

I grabbed a sandwich in the cafeteria and ate it quickly,

then washed my hands and headed upstairs for my equipment.

A short time later, I stepped into the grooming barn and closed the door behind me.

I had miscalculated and, even with eager anticipation for this session, I wasn't early enough to see the ponyboys come around the partition. The three young men were already standing naked under hot water, their wrists bound above, cocks caged, gags placed, with the stable hands doing their work. I stopped dead, mouth going dry, gaze immediately captured by the slimmest ponyboy bound between the other two.

Puck was facing the other way, but I would recognize that sweet plum of an ass anywhere. My mouth pooled with saliva as I watched Liv rub the loofa aggressively over Puck's back and buttocks as if she were a prison warden—rough and pragmatic. From his little grunts of pleasure, I could tell he was enjoying himself.

She noticed me and smiled. "Oliver. You'd better get your stuff out. We'll be done soon."

"Sure. Sorry I'm late."

I fumbled with my gear as my gaze kept returning to delicious Puck under the shower. Finally, I slotted the Canon into the holder on my tripod.

The very moment I looked at the viewer to make sure the camera was aimed properly, Puck turned his head, his gaze pinning me with an energy I tried to decipher. It was the old Puck, the one who seemed angry at everything, gazing at me with his chin held high, his short hair plastered to his head, the ball gag spreading that beautiful mouth.

All the breath left my body as my dick jerked in my shorts, and I recalled feeling those lips around me that very morning.

I lifted my gaze from the viewer and met Puck's angry stare with a similar force. I wasn't backing down. I knew this was either a way he responded instinctively to submission, or a personal quirk that made those moments of sweetness even more valuable.

He turned his gaze away as Liv ran the loofah over the rest of his body. Perhaps he was embarrassed to have me see him like this. But he knew I would have to photograph him in the grooming barn and the stables as part of the agreement I had made with Adam. Hopefully, it wouldn't alter the affection growing between us. But I couldn't worry about that. I had a job to do.

I focused on the other two ponyboys, although it was torture to ignore Puck, especially with water coursing over his pale skin and the way he looked while bound to the ceiling of the grooming barn by his slim wrists. I got close-ups of other bare arms and legs, caged cocks and wrists in bondage, all while my heart pounded and memories of my morning encounter with Puck cycled through my brain.

"All right, Puck darling, let's get you outfitted," Liv said.

I lifted my gaze from the viewer and watched as Liv released Puck's captive arms and led him to stand by the table. She glanced at the whiteboard and did a double take.

"Hmm."

I glanced at the board, found Puck's name and drifted my gaze over Kamal's written instructions: "Basic plus rope halter (red) and tail (black)".

I blinked hard and felt my cock swell as I recalled Kamal's words to me this morning.

Holy fucking hell.

My suddenly clammy hands trembled as I prepared to photograph what was about to happen—hopefully without the camera sliding out of my excited grip.

I took a deep breath as Puck scanned the whiteboard. His eyes widened and he swivelled his head to look at me, cheeks flushing and muscles tensing. His gaze moved to Liv with something like panic in his expression.

"It's okay, sweetheart. You've had the tail before, and the halter's not a big deal. It's not a bridle so there isn't a bit."

She petted Puck gently on his shoulder and walked to the cabinet, opening a drawer and shuffling stuff around before retrieving a bundle of red rope that was knotted to steel rings to make headgear resembling a horse's halter.

She held it up in front of Puck. "See? It's nothing, really. Just makes you look like a pretty pony for Kamal. And"—she glanced my way—"anyone else who might be looking."

I stared at the viewer, embarrassed, because I couldn't fucking wait for Puck to seem more pony-like.

He seemed to settle and gave Liv a curt nod.

"Good boy. First, let's get the regular gear on you, okay?"

As she placed Puck's leather harness and pelvic belt, fastening the buckles deftly and quickly, she continued to give him reassuring strokes and pats to make sure he was all right.

I had to give it to the BCR. Their employees were consistently kind, efficient and perceptive—and so very professional, even in this kinky, boundary-pushing, kind of environment.

Once he had his regular gear on, Liv picked up the rope halter.

"Okay?" she asked. "It's really not a big deal. I promise."

Puck stared at the halter, his gaze sliding to me, then back to Liv. After a moment of hesitation, he nodded.

I straightened and watched overtop of the camera, because I had promised not to identify any of the ponyboys in my images, and Puck wasn't masked as he would be in the pony show. So I stood there, pretending to fiddle with my settings but watching as Liv placed the halter over Puck's brown hair and rested the rope pieces over his forehead and behind his ears. Another red strap came up under his chin to connect to the ones in front of his ears on each side.

The soft red bondage rope used to form the halter looked incredible against Puck's hair and pale skin. Kamal had been right to specify the color, although black would have looked good, too.

"How does that feel?" Liv had removed Puck's ball gag in order to fit the harness. "You can speak."

He frowned but said, "Fine," in a chastened voice. He was behaving himself like a good little ponyboy, and I drank it up because I knew once he was with Kamal his attitude might change.

I wonder if he'd be a good ponyboy for me?

The thought came from nowhere and took the breath out of me. I pushed it aside because if I focused on *that*, I wouldn't have a hope of concentrating on photography or anything else.

Liv had Puck open his mouth so she could place the ball of the gag between his teeth. His gaze kept flitting to me, and I couldn't tell if me watching made him uneasy or excited. I glanced at his cock in its steel cage and it, at least, seemed on board—swelling and straining in its confines.

"All right. Bend over the table now," Liv directed, finding the ponytail designated for Puck in the drawer and holding it up for him.

Puck's chest, framed by the leather straps of his harness, rose and fell rapidly, like he was starting to freak out.

"It's okay. You've had your tail before. It's going to look so pretty, you know." Liv winked at me as she settled Puck once again with her kind words and practical manner.

This time he didn't look at me. He fixed his gaze on the table and frowned as he obeyed Liv's instructions.

I couldn't help a tiny gasp escaping me as he folded himself fluidly over the edge of the table, presenting his backside to Liv and the others in the room. Adrian, who had finished tacking Andrew and was working on Justin, glanced over.

"Ooh, that's a perfect ass, Puck. Don't worry about showing it off."

I silently agreed, my gaze transfixed by Puck's gorgeous globes as Liv gloved up and prepared the tail for insertion.

I pretended to be unaffected as she used the fingers of her free hand to part Puck's cheeks and then pressed the tip of the plug against his sweet, pink hole.

"Open. I'll be gentle and slow," she murmured.

Puck had been facing away from me but now he twisted his head around and pinned me with a hooded stare as Liv eased the tip of the plug into his ass.

I met his stare as my lips parted and a noise escaped me, covered quickly with the pretence of clearing my throat. Then I tore away and watched the plug spread him. When I met his gaze again, the look rattled me as I tried not to dissolve into a million needy pieces.

"You should get some shots of this, Oliver," Liv commented. "Why don't you come closer?"

Oh fuck.

"Yeah. Yes. Good idea." I said, clearing my throat again and grabbing my handheld.

Focus, focus. This is your job. Treat it like one.

I moved in close to where Liv stood at Puck's hip. The plug was halfway in, and I lifted my camera and focused on that, forgetting about that hot gaze and the memories from this morning. I clicked images of the plug seating itself between Puck's cheeks, ignoring his gasps, while Liv's gloved fingers adjusted it and draped the horsehair over his thighs. I hoped my heavy breathing wasn't too obvious.

"Stand up and face the showers."

Puck obeyed, rising gracefully with his back to me so I could get photos of him in all his glory, with the harness and armbands and collar, small glimpses of red rope harness and the buckle of the gag at the back of his head. His bare feet made him seem even more vulnerable and I took several shots of them against the wood of the grooming barn floor.

Liv brought over his socks and boots. "Turn around and put on your trotters, Puck."

Puck did so, swivelling in place with the fluidity of a dancer. Now I could see the soft red rope framing his face, the ball of the gag between his lips, the shiny slide of drool over his chin, and those expressive, desire-filled eyes that seemed to have a direct line to my soul and other, baser places.

As he bent to put on the grey work socks, and then the Doc Marten boots, I took photo after photo. Close-ups of his fingers on the laces, his bent head, and full body shots of him while his face was hidden. When he stood before me again, now in all his ponyboy gear, I lowered the camera and just stared.

"You are so fucking beautiful."

I'd said it without thinking, without caring for a moment who was witness to this declaration. It was my truth and my reality, and why should I deny those feelings?

All eyes turned to me as the blood heated my cheeks. Puck made a choking noise and coughed, but his gaze remained alert and intent. He looked away but came back to me, blushing but not shying away from my interest.

"I can't argue with you, there," Liv commented, taking pity on me and pretending this happened every day.

I regretted it now, because we were supposed to be keeping secrets. So I kept my damn mouth shut and simply watched as the last ponyboy was outfitted and the three men were led out of the grooming barn.

"You okay, Oliver?" Adrian asked, when we were alone.

"Yeah."

"That Puck is an interesting fellow," Adrian said, picking up a cloth that had fallen and placing it back on the table. "Pretty as a picture but nasty in the paddock. Or so I've heard."

I licked my lips, playing it cool. "I've seen him with

Kamal. It's true."

Adrian laughed. "Still. I like a spicy ponyboy."

I narrowed my eyes and must have channelled some big *keep-away-from-my-boy* energy because Adrian raised his hands and shook his head.

"Don't worry. I've got a boyfriend. That one's all yours. If you can handle him."

"I'm sorry, I didn't mean to assume." I ran my free hand through my hair and blew out a puff of air. "I'm not used to feeling this way about...about anyone. Especially about a kinky, gorgeous, oppositional kid with issues."

"Puck has issues?"

"So says Adam."

"Hmm. Maybe Puck's issue is simply Kamal and Kamal's brand of control."

"Maybe."

I started disassembling my tripod. When I was all packed up, I bid Adrian goodbye and headed out to find Kamal and Puck. I didn't want to waste any time, since Kamal had specifically put Puck into that fancy gear for me and my camera.

Lorraine was training Justin, whose inky skin already glistened with sweat, in the corral. I gave her a wave before walking over to lean on the fence of the paddock and watch

Kamal and Puck. I was so overcome by all that had occurred today, I needed to get a grip on myself before I got any closer.

I watched them together, and I could already tell Puck was giving Kamal attitude. He didn't like wearing the tail. Or, he *did* like it, but hated how much he liked it.

When Kamal noticed me, he waved. He gave Puck a slap on the rear to propel him on another circle of the paddock.

"Oliver," Kamal said as he neared.

"Kamal."

Kamal flourished an arm at where Puck trotted with some attempt at speed and grace along the edge of the enclosure. "So? What do you think? He looks pretty good kitted out like that, hmm?"

I raised my eyebrows. "Pretty good is an understatement."

Kamal shrugged. "I see you appreciate the aesthetic."

"Ah, fuck," I swore. "I'm already gone for him. What the fuck am I gonna do, Kamal?"

Kamal gazed at me with affection and skepticism. "That didn't take long. I hope you know what you're getting into."

"Probably not. But I can't seem to help myself."

Kamal watched his recalcitrant ponyboy, now slowing as he neared us and not putting as much effort into his form.

"Fair enough. Do you want me to set up any particular shots for you this afternoon? He may be itching to show off."

Puck returned to Kamal, scowling as much as he could with a ball gag in his mouth, and stopped in front of us, breathing hard and drooling. His hair was already damp with sweat, and the sheen on his skin glistened in the afternoon sun. I was pretty sure Puck had heard Kamal's last remark.

I shook my head. "I'd rather just take candids today, I think."

"Don't forget, the first pony show is on Saturday."

"Looking forward to it."

"Will you do me a favour?"

"Sure."

"I want to impress upon young Puck here, that he is a paddock pony and, thus, not possessed of a free spirit—a pretty pet and nothing more." Kamal grinned. "If you would come in here and examine him—" My eyes widened and I started to decline but Kamal kept speaking. "—a cursory examination, Oliver. You won't need gloves."

Still, I wasn't sure if that was a good idea. But Kamal was the boss in this paddock. I bowed to his authority as a secret part of me thrilled to the prospect of getting my hands on the beautiful, captive man.

"Sure."

"Get in here, then," Kamal said, whipping a leather lead from his pocket and attaching it to the ring on the chin strap of Puck's rope halter.

I slipped through the fence and stood beside them. "What do you want me to—"

"Stand," Kamal said to Puck, who widened his stance and lifted his chin, gaze moving off me to some object in the distance as he quivered with emotion. "Steady."

Kamal reached out and took my hand, laying it on Puck's shoulder. "Just touch him. However you like, but stay away from intimate areas, if you don't mind. Baby steps. He needs to learn to tolerate others. Not just me."

"Okay," I said, my heart pounding and sweat gathering on my nape.

"Pretend you're in the market for a strong, beautiful pony. You want to assess its muscle tone, the smoothness of its coat, check for any problems." Kamal paused for effect. "So you can make an appropriate offer. Hypothetical, of course."

I cleared my throat. "Uh-huh."

I really hoped Puck wouldn't hold this against me. I let my fingers trace over his leather harness and along his side as he continued to avoid my gaze. Mine followed my hand where it drifted over his skin and across the swell of his belly over the pelvic strap. Puck's muscles tightened, and his pores pebbled as I did so. His breath hitched, and he seemed filled with tension.

I couldn't deny the pleasure I received from being able to touch him at Kamal's command and knowing this was all a part of what Puck had signed on for. The fact that he and I had begun a clandestine interaction outside of his role at the ranch only added to my excitement. I could only hope he felt the same. The last thing I wanted to do was ruin what delicate thing was happening between us. But it would take a stronger man than me to resist Kamal's request and refusing it might have seemed suspicious.

I circled around Puck, who stood still as a statue, the only movement in the tension of his jaw. This entire situation was a study in submission and objectification, and I didn't want to disappoint either of them.

My hand drifted over Puck's hip and along the curve of his ass to the delicate crease where it met his thigh. He shuddered.

"You can touch his tail if you like. Just not the plug."

I nodded, unable to speak as I threaded my fingers

through the long black hairs of the tail that cascaded over the backs of Puck's thighs. He made a sound low in his throat.

"Easy. Good pony. Stay still," Kamal encouraged. "You're doing very well."

I glanced at Kamal. "Is this what you want?"

Kamal laughed. "Well, you can be a little rougher. He might like it."

My gaze jerked to Kamal's.

"He's an animal, Oliver. Touch him like one."

Kamal placed one hand under Puck's chin and raised it higher, exposing his long throat. He cupped his other hand around the ponyboy's neck, keeping Puck's head angled back and his gaze forced to the sky.

"Now, examine him. Don't hurt him, obviously, but you don't have to be so gentle. You're trying to assess him, re-member?"

"Fuck. Fine."

I was breathing hard now, but I did as Kamal asked and cupped that beautiful ass in my hands, squeezing Puck's firm glutes as he growled under his breath, pinned in Kamal's grip and subject to my touch.

"Fuck," I said again, moving my palms over Puck's hips to glide up his belly and abdomen, so I could brush my fingers over his nipples and squeeze his pectoral muscles where they were framed by the harness. I was standing close enough to smell the tang of his sweat and hear his quickened breathing.

"So? What do you think?"

"Incredible," I breathed. "His muscle tone is... It's perfect."

Hearing my own words, I started to panic. I needed to get away from what this was doing to me. It was fucking with my body and my head. I was loving it, and I didn't know what that said about me, except that I wanted this boy with my heart and soul, and I was starting to feel like I would die if I couldn't get closer than this.

"All right, Oliver, that's good. Thank you," Kamal said as if aware of my struggle.

I backed up and glanced at Puck's face. His eyes were wide as he stared upward, cheeks flushed and jaw tight. He strained to be still in Kamal's strict hold.

When Kamal removed his hand from Puck's throat, the ponyboy's head lowered into a more natural position, and his gaze met mine with a raw desire that surprised me. He seemed desperate for more, whereas I was terrified of wanting that.

"Thank Oliver for the excellent examination, Puck,"

Kamal said, as he unbuckled the gag and removed it.

Puck licked his lips and moved his jaw before saying, in a rough voice, "Thank you, Oliver."

I didn't know what to do. Was I supposed to reply?

"You're welcome."

Puck's lips curved into a saucy grin as Kamal took his lead and led him away.

I stood there for a long moment, watching them. Then I walked back to the main house fighting a hard-on that didn't want to go away and an ache in my gut that required more than physical intimacy to soothe it.

CHAPTER NINE

CONFIDENCES

OR

SHENANIGANS IN AN EMPTY BUNKHOUSE.

AT SUPPER, PUCK grabbed my hand and pulled me around the corner of the main house, out of sight of the crowd of hungry people.

"That shit in the paddock today...almost killed me," he said before splaying his hand against my chest and attacking my mouth with his.

I wrapped my fingers around his forearm as I kissed him back, telling him with every fibre of my being that I couldn't be *good* anymore. I needed him. I was tired of waiting, and wanting, and touching simply to touch.

When we finally broke apart, the sound of our heavy breaths was loud in the evening air, while a subdued hum of conversation came from around the corner.

"Tell me where," I said, clutching at him.

"The bunkhouse. Nobody's there right now."

"What about upstairs?" I suggested, because it was closer, but that would blow our cover for sure.

"No. Follow me in ten minutes. Pretend to get something to eat, then slip away. Can you do that?"

I nodded. "Sure. Yeah. Of course."

He kissed me again, cupping the bulge in my pants as I groaned. Then he was gone.

When I came back around the corner of the main house, I almost bumped smack into Adam who pressed a drink into my hand.

"Oliver! How are things going?" he asked.

I smiled, trying to stand in a way that wouldn't make my erection obvious.

"Great! I've gotten some pretty amazing photographs

over the past few days."

"And are you feeling comfortable with things?"

"Sure. Yeah."

So comfortable, in fact, I was about to meet a ponyboy in the bunkhouse for shenanigans...if I could get away from Adam.

"Good. The pony show is on Saturday. I'm sure you'll have lots of opportunities there for some incredible photos."

"Can't wait!" I said, praying for him to leave me alone.

He gestured to the table where food was being laid out.

"Supper's on. Don't wait too long, or it will all be gone," he said, as he headed for the buffet.

I slunk around the corner again before anyone else could waylay me. I waited a few minutes, then casually started walking along the trail to the bunkhouse. I was tempted to look back, to see if anyone was watching, but I resisted the urge. Because I honestly didn't fucking care at this point.

My pace increased the farther I got from the main house. When I figured no one could see me, I started jogging. My heart pounded and my entire body zinged with anticipation. I didn't care if he wanted to fuck or just do what we'd done last time. I was up for anything that let me get my hands on him, out of sight of anyone else on this crowded ranch.

The open door of the bunkhouse, normally closed to keep the bugs out and the cooler air inside, beckoned me once I got close enough to see it. I hastened forward and hurried up the steps, stopping dead when I saw Puck laid out on one of the bottom bunks, completely *buck-fuck-naked*, with his legs spread, knees bent, and his dick in hand.

"What took you so long?" he said, teasing the ring in his lip with the tip of his tongue and looking like an angel cast down from heaven.

"Jesus fucking Christ," I said. "Don't move. *Fuck*."

"Close the door before the mosquitos get me," he said. "And latch it."

I did, then stood there—without my camera for once—memorizing every angle to store in my memory. Each tiny mole on his pale skin—the way his bare feet rested on the mattress—the look in his hooded eyes as he gazed at me. His cock was the least interesting thing to me at that moment.

Then one knee fell to the side and he stretched out, displaying himself in the empty confines of the abandoned bunkhouse. Giving himself to me, in whatever way I wanted.

I ran trembling fingers through my hair. He let go of his dick. It flopped against his belly and left a smear of clear fluid behind as he trailed the fingers of one hand to the ring in his right nipple and tugged it.

I made a noise—half whimper, half moan—and moved forward, dropping to my knees on the floor. Glancing at his cock, which seemed very interested in whatever I might do, I put my hand on Puck's throat, covering that slim, vulnerable spot with some very slight pressure, just to let him know I had him, and he was *mine*.

He cursed softly and tilted his head toward me, lips parting in readiness. I captured his mouth as a desperate, needy sound emerged from my throat. He opened beneath my questing tongue and gave me his—tentative and passive. He let me control the kiss, and that gave me the courage to continue. I wanted everything but I needed him to give it willingly.

I increased the pressure on his windpipe just enough to make him gasp and struggle, then I drifted my fingers down to his nipple ring, which I toyed with as he groaned and shuddered beneath me.

"Oliver. Jesus," he gasped, "I need—"

"What? What do you want?"

"Fuck, anything. I'll take anything. I'll *do* anything."

He rose up on one elbow, pulling the T-shirt from my jeans and sliding his hand up my torso. Another curse left his lips.

I inhaled a shaky breath and released him, standing and backing up. He watched me with blown pupils and a blatant curiosity that thrilled and satisfied me. When he was in the paddock his attention was on Kamal—now he was focused on *me*.

I sat on the bunk across from his, and he frowned.

"What are you doing?" He glanced at the door. "We don't have much time."

I pulled my T-shirt off over my head and threw it at him. "I only want to watch," I said.

He blinked at me, as if I'd said something crazy. Which, maybe, I had.

"Watch—what?"

"You."

"Me? But you've already seen—"

I nodded. It was true, I'd seen so much already. But only as a secondary observer. This time I wanted it all *for me*.

"Jerk off into my shirt."

He stared at me, then glanced down at the bunched-up cotton beside him. "Fuck."

"*Now*. We don't have much time, remember?"

"I thought you'd want to bone me."

"I do want to bone you. But right now, I want to watch

you jerk off for me."

"But then—"

I stood up, popping the button of my jeans and sliding the zipper down. "Then you're going to swallow my cock until you're hard again."

"*Then* you'll fuck me?"

"No."

His hand was on his dick in a second. I pulled my cock out and aimed it at him, smiling. "If you put on a good show, I won't make you wait *too* long."

He was already groaning as he pulled on himself, using his pre-ejaculate as lube. But he needed more slide. So I stepped over there, leaned over, and hocked up some spit, dribbling it onto his fingers.

"Oh...God," he moaned, using my saliva to slick himself as I dropped another glob at the top of his balls. He scooped it up quickly, gazing at me with wide eyes as his breaths shortened.

"Look at me," I said. "Look at me when you come."

I fell to my knees again, cock in hand, jerking myself slowly while I watched him. He was vulnerable and glorious in his self-pleasuring. In the paddock, Kamal had all the control. Now Puck took it, albeit under my directions, and it was beautiful to see him give himself the pleasure he craved.

"Oh yes, get yourself off, my beautiful, contrary ponyboy. Jerk that gorgeous cock for me."

His hand flew on his dick, as his neck stretched out. His eyes closed.

"I'm close. Oh fuck, I'm close," he panted, lips shiny from his tongue. He couldn't stop moistening them.

"Open your eyes. Look at me."

He did so, a dark flush spreading over his collarbone and rising to the tips of his ears.

"Say my name."

Puck's breath hitched, and he started to come as he groaned out, "Oliver! Oliver, ah, *Oliver.*"

I smiled, delighted to watch him satisfy himself with my name on his lips. He grabbed my T-shirt and pressed it against his cock as he continued to ride the aftershocks of his orgasm, pressing his face into the mattress and giving over to it.

I whipped off my shoes and shorts, leaving them on the bunk, and covered him with my body, kissing his neck and his shoulder as he sank, sated into the mattress.

"That was hot," he whispered.

"So hot."

I pressed my erection against the small of his back and

he turned his head to me.

"You can fuck me," he said.

I grinned. "I know."

He didn't reply, just arched his back and bumped up against me. "Will you?"

"Not today." It was funny. I'd been so desperate to get Puck alone, but having intercourse was something I wanted to wait for. I didn't want to do it on the fly, when we didn't think we had much time. Somehow, some way, we'd find a place where we could take it slow.

"What? Why not?"

But I didn't say that, in case he thought I was being too romantic. Maybe all Puck wanted was a quick fuck against the wall. But I'd been there and done that with other men, and something made me want to wait.

"I'm not ready. And I like making you wait."

"Bastard. I hate you." He splayed out beneath me, all fight gone, the afterglow of his orgasm making him soft and boneless.

"No you don't," I said, pushing my cock against his smooth buttock, leaving a wet trail, teasing him with it.

"You're killing me."

"You like it."

"Fuck."

"Getting hard again?"

"Yes."

"Wow."

He laughed, rolling over to show me. "See?"

"You are a perfect, beautiful little slut."

"Fuck, Oliver. Say that again."

I grinned and leaned down to lick over his jaw. "You are—" I licked over his Adam's apple. "—a beautiful—" I licked the perfect lobe of his ear. "—little—" I licked the tip of his nose, making him laugh. I leaned in to whisper in his ear. "—slut."

He groaned, arching up against me, almost fully hard again as he pulled at himself. "Fuuuuck. Shit."

I sat back on my heels and waved my dick at him. "You want this?"

"Yeah," he said, scrabbling to his knees and grabbing my chin as he kissed me, fierce and possessive, like he wasn't completely at my mercy. He smiled against my mouth. "I like the way you talk."

"Good. I like to tell you what to do."

"Tell me what to do now."

I pushed gently on his shoulder, guiding him to my cock. "I want to fuck your mouth."

"God. Okay."

"I like to watch you choke on it."

"You're a pervert, Oliver," he said, with a sigh.

"Maybe."

"Between you and Kamal, I don't know what to do."

"Do what you're told, Puck."

"Oliver," he sighed and opened his mouth as I guided my cock between his lips.

"Good boy."

He choked a laugh, the vibrations riding my dick, making me groan and curse. I held him steady while I thrust into his hot, wet heat, his tongue flat and broad beneath me, his gaze holding mine.

"Oh, Jesus. Puck. *Puck*," I stuttered, using him to pleasure myself, remembering everything I'd seen him do for Kamal and how he'd bristled and fought but now was a pliant plaything for *me*. The power I seemed to have over him was heady, and I knew he could withdraw it in an instant. The only hold I had on him was his desire for me. But that was enough. For now.

I thrust deeper, making him choke again, and then I came hard, gripping his shoulder and emptying into his willing throat as he made the most delicious sounds.

This time, he swallowed everything.

Finally, he pulled off and licked his lips, giving me the most lascivious grin as his hand drifted down to grab his erection.

"Mmm. So good," I hummed.

I stared down at him as he lazily stroked himself, while I caught my breath and relished the quiet privacy of the bunkhouse.

I glanced at the door and then back at Puck. "How much time you think we have?"

He glanced at the door, too, and shrugged. "Maybe half an hour? If we're lucky."

I nodded. I knew what I wanted.

"Get up and sit on the bunk."

He cocked his head. "My, you get bossy when a boy lets you fuck his mouth."

I gave a soft laugh and offered my hand to help him. "I like being bossy with you."

"I noticed."

Puck sat his bare ass on the bunk and leaned back, propping himself on one hand while he teased himself with the other and gazed up at me.

"What do you want, Oliver?"

I didn't answer, simply tucked myself away and dropped to my knees, sliding my hands along his thighs and over his hips as I leaned toward his dick.

He grinned, aiming it at me with his eyebrows arched. "This?" he whispered.

"Yeah."

"You mean I don't have to do it myself?"

"Nope."

He smiled, increasing the rhythm of his strokes as I bent forward and kissed his dick softly on its glistening head.

Puck whimpered and his breath hitched again. "Oliver..."

I met his gaze and opened my mouth, engulfing his cock and swirling my tongue over it.

"Oh! *Fuck,*" he groaned, lowering his hand and leaning back on both arms now as he gave himself up to me. "Oh, God."

His hips moved unconsciously forward.

I wrapped my fingers around the base of his dick, holding it firmly as I used my tongue and jaw to force the most erotic, soul-destroying sounds from him. He tasted of sweat and spunk and testosterone, those earthy notes pulling at me with sweet seduction as I went to town on him, clutching his hips to keep him still.

He tried to thrust, but I increased the strength of my hold and he whined. The look of frustration on his face, warring with the bliss of having his dick sucked, entranced me. He stilled and suffered while I went at him–licking and sucking him everywhere, my tongue dipping down to his balls and taint before running up the underside of his cock again.

He curled forward, fingers circling behind my head and pushing me forward gently. He was tired of being the passive one, and he let me know it by gripping my hair and controlling the movements of my head.

I growled and increased my sloppy, drooling attack, relishing the sounds that came from his parted lips—more urgent and breathless as he approached his climax. Once I relaxed my grip on his hips, he began to fuck my face with abandon, holding my head still and pushing his cock to the back of my throat like I'd done to him moments ago.

Electric tingles coursed through me as I let him use me, until, with a cry, he stilled and emptied with a grunt. His grasp pulled at my scalp as I swallowed his release with satisfaction and triumph.

"Oh...my...*fuck!*" he gasped, his hold on my hair changing from a death grip to a caress as he came down from his ecstatic climax. I tightened my arms around his hips and sucked him through the waning of his orgasm until he squirmed and pushed me off.

"Stop. God, stop. Too much."

I relinquished him with a sadness I felt to my toes because I knew the time we'd had together was about to run out. I lay my head on his thigh and closed my eyes, enjoying the feel of his fingers threading softly through my hair.

The bunkhouse was silent and still.

"Oliver," he said, finally.

I looked up at him, my heart melting at how wrecked and serene he looked.

"Let's go for a swim."

I hadn't expected him to say that. I thought he'd dismiss me with the excuse that the others would be back, and I'd have to leave out of politeness.

So I blinked in surprise and said, "Sure," then stood shakily. I watched Puck pull on a pair of shorts and a T-shirt, then slide into his flip-flops.

"I don't have my suit," I said.

"Good." He winked. "'Cause I'm not bringing mine."

I smiled, wondering what we'd do if any of the other guys decided a swim would be nice. But honestly, I didn't care. We were at a kink ranch, for God's sake. Pretty sure everyone could handle a couple of bare asses and some satisfied junk hanging out.

We got out of the bunkhouse before anyone returned from the main house. Puck led me along another narrow trail through the woods, glancing back to make sure I was keeping up and, at one point, taking my hand to pull me gently along. He seemed excited to show me the beach, where I hadn't as yet spent any time.

I was simply happy to be with him.

"Come on. It's not much farther."

"Okay."

I felt like I was at summer camp, following an enchanting new friend through the woods to a secret spot, where we would sit and speak about daring things and giggle at how dumb we thought the straight boys were—that surreptitious sense of sharing something private and exciting. My friendships at camp had been innocent but intense, and I'd crushed on a few boys during those idylls.

Now I was an adult, following my newest crush along a forest path, after having gotten each other off in an empty bunkhouse on a pony-play ranch. The trees and insects were the only witnesses to our smug glances and secret smiles.

After a short time, we emerged to the wide expanse of

the lake and a small strip of sand. The waning sun sparkled on the top of the water like diamonds.

There was a floating dock about twenty feet out. Puck was already taking off his clothes.

"Coming in?"

"Sure," I said, getting naked and following Puck into the cool water.

He waded in up to his hips, then put his hands together and dived forward, swimming out to the dock with bold, sure strokes.

I followed.

Puck glanced behind him with a grin. "Come on, Oliver. Keep up, will you?"

I smiled as I went deeper, the sand on the bottom of the lake squishing between my toes. I was a city boy at heart and uneasy in open water. But the draw Puck had on me was strong, and I pushed past my discomfort and dived, swimming out to where he had pulled himself onto the floating platform.

If I'd needed motivation, the sight of Puck's slim form as he heaved himself onto the undulating dock and stood, sleek muscles bunching and releasing, water sluicing off his skin, hair slicked to his head, was enough.

He turned, standing there like Michelangelo's David, his

cock flaccid for once, hands on his hips, self-satisfied look on his face, watching me.

"Oh, good, you can swim," he said.

I gained the wooden edge of the platform and folded my arms, resting my chin on them, gazing up at him. *Fuck.* He was glorious.

He crouched down, unashamed of his nudity—bits dangling right in front of me—as he patted the top of my head and clicked his tongue. "You kept up. Now, are you staying in there, or coming out?"

"Coming out. The water's cold."

"Poor you. Come on, then."

He stood and gave me room to haul myself up and onto the platform. Puck sat down beside me, and we dangled our legs in the water, gazing back at the shoreline.

"This is...something," I said, gesturing around us. The evening chorus of birds and insects lulled my already relaxed brain into a state of pure contentment. The fact I had a gorgeous boy beside me who seemed to enjoy my company made my surroundings that much more special.

But now we weren't actively trying to fuck each other—for the moment—there was a lull in conversation.

Then Puck said, "I came here to get away from it all."

I glanced at him, observing a crease in his forehead before he looked away and scratched at a spot above his knee.

"Yeah?"

He glanced at me, assessing, maybe deciding if he wanted to continue—if he trusted me enough to share.

"Yeah." He nodded. Then puffed a soft laugh. "I'm supposed to be in Munich."

That was not what I had expected.

"What? Really?"

He swatted a fly away from his face. "I was supposed to go visit my brother. He's a researcher at a hospital there."

"Oh." I waited for him to say something else. When he didn't, I probed gently. "You didn't want to go?"

He shook his head. "I needed to be...by myself. Well, not by myself, obviously," he gestured at me. "But away from the people who know about everything."

I nodded, not understanding yet, but to show I was here for him. Since we had no connection beyond the BCR, maybe he felt he could unburden himself. I didn't know whether to ask for clarification or just be quiet. I chose the easier option. And, after a little while, he started speaking again.

"My best friend...he's so pigheaded," Puck said quietly, shaking his head in frustration. "I told him the guy he was seeing was a dick, and he didn't listen. This boy he liked—the loser he was *obsessed* with—was *using*, and so fucking *irresponsible*. I warned him, but he ignored me. He thought I was jealous or something, which is really turned around."

I listened to the hum of cicadas and the occasional call of a loon while I sat there, a listening ear for whatever he wanted to get off his chest.

"Fucker crashed the car they were in. This boy, this stupid, fucking *kid*, was on a cocktail of drugs and crashed the car, *killing* himself and landing my best friend in the hospital, fighting for his life."

"Oh shit. That's terrible." My words sounded so ineffectual, but I couldn't think of anything else to say. "Is your friend...is he all right?"

"Depends on your definition of *all right*."

"I'm so sorry."

"Yeah, everybody's sorry. Doesn't help."

"Aw, Puck. Jesus."

"Just let me talk. I haven't talked about any of this. And I think I need to."

CHAPTER TEN

A MIDSUMMER NIGHT'S DREAM

OR

PONYBOYS ON PARADE

PUCK STARED AT the lake, his knuckles white where they grasped the edge of the dock, as I waited for him to say more.

"He's in the hospital with a fractured spine. He may never walk again," Puck said, swirling his calves in the water. "Name's Elijah."

A chill ran through me, and it wasn't just the wetness

drying on my skin. I almost said "I'm sorry" again, but I kept my mouth shut. There was nothing I could say as an outsider that wouldn't sound clichéd or ring hollow.

As a photographer, I was used to quietly observing things, listening to conversations and judging when to give input. Often, I decided it was wiser to wait and watch and simply record what was happening. I found the photographs I'd taken when I'd kept myself removed from what was going on evinced truth and immediacy. It was a useful skill.

Puck turned and I met his gaze, trying to show with my expression that even though I couldn't possibly understand what he was going through I cared and wanted to take some of the weight off him. Even if simply as a sounding board—a way for him to say these things out loud, instead of keeping them hidden inside him.

"I'm just so—so *fucking* angry. Because I told him this kid was dangerous and was going to get him killed. And he didn't fucking *listen* to me!"

Puck's breath hitched, and he made a noise like a sob that he strangled as soon as it tried to escape.

"I know that's the wrong thing to be thinking. I should be sympathetic and helpful, when all I want to do is kill this stupid kid that did this to him, but I can't because the kid is already dead from his own fucking stupidity. And Elijah is never going to be the same. And neither am I." He turned to me, his gaze filled with anger and despair. "And it's just not fucking fair, Oliver."

I reached out because it was the only thing that seemed remotely appropriate. I wrapped an arm around him and pulled him against me.

He stiffened for a moment, and I thought I'd made a mistake. But then he melted against me, nuzzled into my neck and shuddered, gasping deep breaths and shaking with some violent emotion. It didn't matter if it was rage or hopelessness or grief. Whatever it was, he'd pushed it down for so long it was killing him from the inside.

"I don't—" he gasped. "I'm sorry—" he said, before a sob wracked him and he struggled to get away. "Fuck!"

I relaxed my hold and watched him pull from my embrace. His legs thrashed, splashing in the water. He seemed startled to be allowed to break free. His hand flew to his face, fingers swiping at his eyes as his shoulders heaved.

"No, Oliver," he moaned as he reached out and grabbed me, lurching into my willing arms.

A surge of emotion overcame me, and I pulled him into my embrace again, held him firmly around his bare waist, and whispered nonsense into his ear. "It's okay, Puck. I know. You're okay." His skin was covered in goose pimples and still slippery with lake water.

I half expected him to pull away again, but I wasn't sure I'd be able to let him this time. He felt so good in my arms, and it pleased me to hold him while he fell apart.

Strange, forlorn sounds broke from his throat as he let his pain out. I had no idea what it would be like to see my best friend so damaged and bereft. Especially if I wasn't able to talk about it with anyone. Until I found myself at a kinky pony play ranch, confessing to my latest conquest, who would let me cover him in my tears and snot while sitting naked on clammy wet wood if it would only make me feel better.

I held Puck tight while he shuddered and keened, keeping him close, until after what seemed a very long time, he quieted, sagging against me like an empty sack.

We listened to the lapping of water against the dock and the calls of birds from the lakeshore.

"You okay?" I asked after a while. I genuinely needed to know if he was still conscious or if he'd fallen asleep against my shoulder. His breathing was long and even, and he hadn't made a sound for a while.

"I'm sorry. I'm so sorry."

"No, come on. Something tells me you've needed to do that for quite some time."

He took a deep breath, then let it out. "Maybe. Probably."

I let him sit up. He seemed shy and embarrassed, avoiding my gaze and swiping his cheeks with the back of his hand.

"I probably got you wet."

"I was already wet."

He nodded, gazing over the water.

"Can I ask you something?" I said.

"Sure."

"Your brother in Munich. He knows where you are?"

Puck swung his head to give me a skeptical look. "What? *No.*"

"But you didn't just not show up. He knows you're safe?"

"Oh. Shit, yes. Of course." Puck laughed softly and it was a relief to hear. "Except he thinks I'm at some kind of yoga retreat."

"When I told my buddy I was leaving for a few weeks, that's what he thought too."

Puck's eyes went wide. "Did you tell him where you were *really* going?"

"I did. He was jealous."

Puck chuckled. "Yeah, well. I signed up for this gig and then forgot all about it. The BCR just happened to email me with an available spot shortly after the accident, when I'd already promised my brother I'd visit *him*. My family could tell things were getting to me. But then, this place and this experience, seemed like the best way to forget everything. At least for a little while."

"Is it working?"

"Kind of?" He laughed bitterly. "No. Not really."

I put a comforting hand on his shoulder.

"When I'm in the paddock or the arena with Kamal," he said, shaking his head. "I love every minute of it."

"Really? It doesn't seem like you—"

"But I feel guilty every minute that I'm loving it."

"Ah."

"Because *I* get to play sexy ponyboy for my superhot trainer slash Dom, who, by the way, is much more attractive than I'd anticipated. And Elijah gets to lie in his hospital bed," he cleared his throat, voice thick with emotion. "Gets to lie there and contemplate never being able to walk again."

It all made sense now. This explained why Puck fought Kamal so relentlessly in the paddock. How must it feel to trot around at the whim of his sexy and dominant master, trying to be the most graceful, gorgeous ponyboy, when his best friend might never have use of his legs again?

"Aw, Puck," I said, taking his chin in my hand and kissing him with all the tenderness I could give him, then pulling back. "You've been through a lot."

He shook his head. "Nothing I've had to go through compares to what Elijah's going through right now. And I'm not there to, like, help him or talk to him because I can't fucking bear it."

"It's okay to take a break and get away for a bit."

"Elijah can't take a break. I mean, his family's there, and they're wonderful. I can't even think about how hard this is for *them*."

"You aren't Elijah. Thank God you aren't Elijah. Thank whatever you want—the universe, fate—but instead of feeling guilty for enjoying your life, feel grateful, maybe?"

"Easy to say."

"Yeah. You could talk to Adam."

Puck stared at me. "You think I need therapy?"

"Puck," I said. "Anyone who's gone through what you did could use some counselling. It's not a four-letter word."

"Have you ever?"

"As a matter of fact, yes."

His eyes widened.

"I had issues with anxiety when I was about fourteen, fifteen. Like, major issues. My parents tried to address it, but they signed me up for some counselling, and it helped so much. And, yeah, I was resistant at first. But the anxiety got so bad it was interfering with school and social activities. Therapy made a world of difference."

"Hmm. I don't know if I—" He stared into the distance. A loon called across the shimmering water. "I came here to escape all of that."

"Sure, but you said it wasn't really working?"

"I don't know."

"Look, I'm not telling you to talk to Adam. Just that the option is there. I'm really glad you talked to me. Did it help?"

"I think so. Yeah." He laughed and bumped my knee with his. "Even though I'm so embarrassed I don't know if I can ever see you again."

A lead brick fell into my stomach until I noticed the sparkle in his eye and his soft smile. "Joking. I'm joking."

I put a shaky hand to my forehead. "Don't do that. I thought you meant it."

"Is it that important to you?"

"What? *This?*" I gestured between the two of us.

"Yeah."

"Puck. Yes. I love what's happening here. I don't want it to stop."

He nodded, blushing. "Good. Me either."

The sun was close to setting, so we swam back to shore, got dressed, and headed back to the bunkhouse. We were quiet as we walked through the darkening woods. I felt a real intimacy between us as our footfalls landed in the grass and dirt, and the chirping of crickets and frogs surrounded us.

As we neared the bunkhouse, human voices from inside the panelled walls joined the cacophony of small animals. I took my leave, kissing Puck on his lightly stubbled cheek and squeezing his fingers, before I strode back to the main house in the glistening moonlight.

*

I DIDN'T SEE Puck again until the pony show the following day.

I'd planned to photograph the men being tacked up, but I'd had a software issue with the Nikon camera that took me all morning to sort out. It delayed me so that I barely had time to get to the paddock and set up my tripod and camera by the fence.

It was strange to see the bleachers filled with people of all types; some in fine clothes similar to those worn to an actual equestrian event, others in fetish gear, still more in jeans and T-shirts. They spoke and laughed amongst themselves as they waited for the show to begin, the air filled with excited anticipation.

I was just as eager to see the ponyboys strut their stuff for the crowd. Especially one *particular* ponyboy. Because the afternoon shift was first on the rotation this weekend, I knew Puck would be performing today. There was no way I was missing that.

"Hey, Oliver."

I turned to see Lincoln in skinny red jeans and an *Imagine Dragons* T-shirt, at my elbow.

"Hi. How's it going?"

He tilted his head, giving me a grin. "Good. You?"

"Well, despite having a cock-up of a morning with my camera equipment, fine."

"Oh shit. Got everything working I hope?"

"Yeah. Just in time."

Lincoln appraised me with his gaze. "I know you're supposed to take photos of all of us, but I think you're here to see a particular person."

I pretended confusion. "Hmm? What?"

Lincoln laughed. "I saw you together last night, when you got back from"—he waved his hand in the air—"whatever you were doing."

I cleared my throat and pretended to fiddle with my camera. "We were at the beach. Swimming."

"Okay."

I narrowed my eyes. "Did Puck say anything?"

Lincoln laughed, shaking his head. "Nope. He just got ready for bed. Went to sleep. Easier than he has since he got here."

"Oh?"

"Usually, he tosses and turns all night. But he was out like a light and slept through for once. At least, I think so. Usually, I wake up at least a few times because of his noises."

"Oh."

"I guess the *swimming* did him some good."

I smiled. "Yeah, I guess so. Look, we're trying to keep it quiet..."

He grinned. "So there *is* something going on."

I blinked. I couldn't believe he'd got me. This ranch was hell on my defenses.

"Oh, you're good."

Lincoln preened a bit. "Don't worry. I won't tell anyone. I'm glad for Puck. He may be a headcase with Kamal, but he's very cool with all of us. He's well liked."

I was pleased to hear it, although a tiny stab of jealousy hit me in the chest. I wanted to *claim* Puck. I wanted everyone to know he was mine. Which was such a caveman thing to want I could hardly process it and simply pushed the feeling down.

"Good. And thanks."

"No problem." He gestured to the paddock. "Looks like they're getting started."

Adam came into the ring, dressed in slacks and a white button-down with a bow tie, looking so sexy and put together he took my breath away. As my employer, he was hardly a suitable subject for a romantic attachment, but I would have been sorely tempted if Puck hadn't trumped every other man for whom I'd ever had romantic thoughts.

"Good afternoon, everyone! Welcome to the first pony show of the summer session, here at the Braided Crop Ranch. We have three lovely ponyboys to perform today. In a moment, their trainers will bring them out and have them parade around the ring for you."

Cheers and whistles sounded from the bleachers.

Adam announced the ponies with their show names, saving Puck for last.

"And now, for our final ponyboy, Tempest, with his handsome trainer, Kamal!"

Tempest. It suited Puck perfectly. Even though it referenced the wrong Shakespeare play, since Puck was a character from *A Midsummer Night's Dream,* it certainly fit his fiery nature.

When Tempest trotted out with Kamal, wearing the red rope halter and a fantastic, Elizabethan-type mask in burgundy with gold filigree trim, my mouth went dry. The crowd whooped louder than ever, and Puck carried himself with an effortless grace and a confidence that spoke to the training he'd received.

"He looks amazing," Lincoln commented. "Seems more comfortable too."

"Yeah. *Jesus.*" I lifted a trembling hand to my forehead.

Lincoln glanced at me, then laughed. "You can't hide what you're feeling for him, you know."

I nodded, blushing. "I promised I'd try."

"Fair enough," he said.

The inaugural pony show consisted of the trainers having the ponyboys show off their figures and their gaits by prancing around the ring and eventually jumping over some low oxers. Afterward, they paraded around the ring a last time as Adam requested applause from the captivated audience.

Then the ponyboys were brought outside the paddock to pose for photos with any of the guests who paid for the privilege. A lineup soon formed in front of Tempest in his golden mask, and I couldn't get anywhere near him.

I ended up hanging back and watching from a distance to make sure he was doing okay. Kamal stayed close to Puck and ensured the rules were followed. Nobody was allowed to touch a ponyboy, although they were permitted to stand close for a photo.

How people were able to be near Puck in that get-up and be forbidden to touch him seemed like torture, but I was very glad those rules existed.

He caught my eye several times and we stared at each other while he had his photo taken with various enthusiastic men and women. He looked so majestic and beautiful, and this was only the beginning. In future shows, he and the other ponyboys would wear the full bridles with the metal bits and the flowing tails. I swallowed, recalling how Puck had looked with the black horsehair cascading down the backs of those strong and shapely legs. I wasn't sure I could handle him in full show gear, when seeing him like this was like a physical blow to the heart.

I was thankful I had the use of the tripod during the show since my hands had only recently ceased trembling. It had been a relief, in a way, to be able to capture the sexy ponyboys in full without worrying about identifying features, since they all wore the beautiful masks that disguised their faces and transformed them into fantastical creatures from another universe.

By the time the audience had thinned to only a handful of people speaking with Adam, Kamal caught my eye and beckoned me over. My gut wrenched at the thought of going closer to the object of my extreme desire whilst keeping my true feelings suppressed, but Kamal was difficult to ignore.

When I got there, cradling my camera in sweaty palms, Kamal gestured to Puck.

"So? What do you think of Tempest?"

I cleared my throat. "All the ponyboys looked amazing."

"Yes, but Tempest, my sweet scene-stealer. What do you think of him?"

I blinked, scrambling for something to say that wouldn't betray my true feelings, but would express how stunning Puck really was. Apparently, my wordless answer was enough.

Kamal laughed. "Yes, I can imagine it's difficult to find the words. He performed beautifully. I'm very impressed with how he did today."

I risked a glance at Puck to find him staring at me. Our gazes locked as my body responded to the intensity in his green eyes.

Kamal's gaze drifted back and forth between us.

"Hmm. Something going on here that I'm not aware of?"

I tore my gaze away and acted dumb. "Hmm?"

Kamal examined me and smiled. "That's a good act, Oliver. But you can't fool me."

I shrugged, the heat in my face betraying to Kamal exactly how I felt about his prized ponyboy.

Then Puck said "Leave him alone please" in such a soft voice that we stared at him in surprise.

"I don't want everyone to know. Not yet."

Kamal lifted a hand to touch the edge of Puck's pretty mask and glanced my way.

"So, there *is* something going on between the two of you."

I looked at the ground, feeling guilty, although I had every right to pursue something with Puck. "Yeah."

"Kamal, please don't tell anyone. Let us keep it quiet for a little while," Puck said.

"Why? You're not violating any rules."

"I think," I said, glancing at Puck who seemed uncomfortable with Kamal's scrutiny of, and interest in, his private dalliances. "I think that Puck wants us to fly under the radar for a little while." I ran a hand through my hair, recalling Lincoln's comments from earlier. "Even though I'm not sure we're fooling anyone, to be honest."

Kamal grinned and chucked his ponyboy under the chin. "I hate to tell you, but anyone who watches the two of you together can see the chemistry. And I can fucking *feel* it."

Puck and I swivelled our heads to gape at Kamal, who laughed and passed me Tempest's lead rope.

"Here. Have a moment with him, then take him to the grooming barn. I'm going back to the house."

I stood there, staring at the rope in my hand for several moments as Kamal walked away. Everyone else had gone into the arena or were headed back to the resort, so Puck and I stood alone together in the field.

I looked up and into the prettiest pair of green eyes I knew. Puck watched me from his golden mask, his cheeks flushed from the sun and exertion and probably something else.

"What are you going to do with me?" he said, tongue

flicking the silver ring in his lower lip.

All the blood drained from my upper body and into my lower half as I tried to adjust to the dizzying arousal.

"I'll tell you what I'd like to do with you," I said, barely giving the words volume.

I wasn't sure he'd heard me. He stepped forward, so close I smelled leather and the musk of his sweat.

"Say that again."

Puck's soft breath feathered over my skin as I struggled to remain coherent in the face of a tsunami of lust.

"I'll tell you what I'd like to do with you," I repeated, slightly louder. He was so close now.

We gazed at each other, emotion and need flaring between us like a firestorm.

"What do you want to do with me?" he whispered.

"I want..." I almost choked on the words. "I want—*everything.*"

"I'll give you *everything.* But we're in the middle of a field. It would cause quite the scandal if I gave it to you right this minute."

I smiled briefly at his joke, aroused beyond measure.

"A kiss, then?"

Our faces were only inches apart. Puck seemed like an

otherworldly apparition in his golden mask. He nodded once, then his lips found mine and we kissed—so softly, that I gasped with the tender heat of it. I clamped down on the part of me that wanted to devour him, and instead, cherished the sweetness of this moment.

The kiss affected me, so much so that when Puck pulled back with a sigh, I stood paralyzed and breathless.

"I know a place where we can—" Puck swallowed and licked his lips. "—have some time alone. *Undisturbed.*"

I nodded, afraid to speak.

"Meet me tonight? Outside the bunkhouse. Around eleven?"

I nodded again.

The hint of a smile emerged on his face. I think he was amused at my tortured state.

"You going to be okay?"

"I don't think so."

He laughed and I wrapped trembling fingers around his bicep, feeling the strength of his sinewy muscles.

"I need to take you to the grooming barn."

"Yeah. I'm a mess."

I shook my head. "No. You're not. But I can't fucking deal with the way you look and feel and smell right now. So

I'd better take you there before I make a really bad decision."

He laughed again. "Oliver..."

"Puck. I'm in way over my head, here."

He sobered and gave me such an intense and tender look, I felt it in my bones.

"Take me to the grooming barn, Oliver."

"Okay."

"And meet me at the bunkhouse tonight."

"Okay."

"Promise?"

"Yeah."

CHAPTER ELEVEN

A FOREST HIDEAWAY

OR

DIRTY DEEDS DONE DIRT CHEAP

I COULD BARELY concentrate for the rest of the day. I went through the motions, all the while my head full of feelings and my body a tightrope of desire.

During supper I stayed away from Puck, and he didn't approach me. I was scared to even look his way since I'd been told by two different people our affection for each other was obvious. I made polite conversation with Adam and Lorraine and asked Kamal a few general questions about pony training.

By the time darkness fell, the main house had grown quiet. I went upstairs and lay on my bed, listening to music on my phone and trying to quell my growing excitement. I kept checking the clock.

At ten thirty I pulled the buds from my ears and listened intently to the expansive quiet of the house outside my door. I heard laughter in the distance, and a door shut somewhere. Then there was nothing.

At ten forty-five, I put my phone and earbuds on the bedside table, grabbed the flashlight from its spot on my dresser, and eased my door open. I peeked my head out to make sure the coast was clear.

It was now or never. And never was not an option.

I stepped into the hall and closed the door behind me, locking it as softly as I could and making my way along to the stairs, then heading to the main level. Only the emergency lights were on, giving the place an eerie glow. I managed to make it out the back door with only one squeak of my shoe on the polished floor. Once on the porch, after I'd shut the door, I breathed a sigh of relief.

I checked my bearings to see if anyone else was outside.

The coast was clear, so I descended onto the grass and walked in the direction of the bunkhouse. I didn't turn on my flashlight until I was a good way along the path, so nobody at the main house would see a bouncing light and wonder. I sincerely hoped the guys in the bunkhouse were too busy to pay attention to anything but hijinks and whatever else a group of horny young men might get up to at this time of night.

Part of me was envious that they all got to hang out together in a very cool bunking arrangement. But I probably wouldn't have dealt very well with having to hide my affection for Puck in such close confines, and where he might be—and probably was—approached frequently by other men. If what Lincoln had said was true, and they all knew there was something going on between me and Puck, I hoped it would keep them from approaching him. But I couldn't hope for miracles.

The bunkhouse loomed ahead of me.

I kept my flashlight pointed at the ground so I could see my way but not betray my arrival. As I got close enough that the circle of its light touched the step below the door, I heard a cough. I aimed the beam of the flashlight in that direction, and it landed on a pair of bubble-gum pink Doc Marten's with rainbow laces.

Puck.

The pretty boots started to move toward me as I followed the illumination along the long line of his jeans-clad legs, past the hem of his snug T-shirt, over the Spiderman Logo, up his neck and chin to his sweet smile and glinting, excited eyes, squinting in the bright light.

"You found me," he said.

By now he was right in front of me. I lowered the flashlight so I could bathe in his proximity. I could still see his face, although not clearly in the darkness. But it didn't matter, because in a moment, his lips found mine and caught me up in a surge of heat and desire.

His fingers gently pried the flashlight from my hand.

When he pulled away, he drifted the beam over me from head to foot and made a satisfied sound. "Hell, yes. So hot. Follow me."

I'd worn a pair of ripped jeans, canvas runners, and a faded grey T-shirt with a black-checked button-down open over it to ward off the evening chill. Trying to look younger and maybe not so professional.

Puck reached out and took my hand. I loved the way he took me in hand and put me where I was wanted, as much as I liked the way he gave himself over to me when we got where we were going. I would go just about anywhere with this compelling and confusing young man.

Now we moved through dense brush to the songs of crickets and night birds. I wondered if he had a destination in mind and if there would be anything more than a rocky space on the ground to get up to what we so obviously wanted to do with each other. I held my tongue and trusted that he'd get us where we needed to be.

I watched the beam of the flashlight he held—my flashlight—bob ahead of us. It was spooky, to be honest, and I clutched his hand as if letting go would mean disaster. I cried out when a sudden fluttering of wings and the cry of a small animal sounded nearby.

Puck laughed. "We're almost there. Don't worry."

"I'm not worried," I said, affecting nonchalance, although he could probably feel the clammy sweat on my palm.

"You're trembling," he said.

"How do you know that's not just anticipation?"

"I don't. Anyway, we're here. It's not much but there are four walls and a roof."

The light of his flashlight fell on the scruffy wood walls of a diminutive shack at the end of the very-much-not-really-a-trail we were on.

"Okay. Well, then."

Were there spiders in there? There would probably be spiders. I coughed.

Puck aimed the flashlight on my face. "Oh, come on. You're not worried about a little dirt, are you, Oliver?"

"Of course not."

He looked me up and down. "Oh, good. Because by the time I'm done with you, you're going to be an absolute mess."

Suddenly I didn't care about spiders. That is, I cared about them *a lot* less.

"Okay. Fuck."

He grinned. "Come on."

I followed him to a rickety door that opened with a creak when he pushed on it.

"There's no lock?"

"Who the hell's gonna find us out here?"

We stepped inside, onto wood floorboards that complained immediately.

"Nobody else knows about this place?"

"Well..." Puck shook his head. "Adam was the one who mentioned it. He told me how to find it."

That stopped me short. "Did you tell him what—"

Puck pulled me further into the dank, dark room.

"Yes, exactly. I asked him if he knew of any place I could fuck the shit out of you in private and not under the stars, which was my second choice, honestly."

I didn't say anything. I wasn't sure if he was kidding. He shone the flashlight under his chin, which made him look a little bit scary.

"I didn't say it in those exact words. And I didn't reference you at all. I just asked if there was anywhere a ponyboy could go to get his dick sucked other than the crowded bunkhouse or the lake."

I crossed my arms over my chest and stayed still, not eager to encounter any webs in the darkness.

"Okay. Wow. This place...isn't half bad." I tried to sound optimistic.

"Hold on a second. There's a lantern."

Puck's shoes scuffed against the floorboards as he moved forward.

"Wait, have you already been here?"

Puck laughed. He turned and moved, pressing the length of his body against me, and angled the flashlight away. "No, Oliver. I'm only a slut for you, apparently."

And all I could smell was Puck. All I could feel was Puck. I wrapped my hands around his biceps, keeping him with me, feeling safe when I was near him.

"That makes me happy," I said, sucking on his neck, nuzzling against him. I just wanted to kiss every part of him. He smelled so good.

"I like to make you happy."

I chuckled. "Maybe we should light that lantern. If I'm honest I'm a little scared of spiders."

"I see," Puck said, "Well, luckily, I'm not."

I laughed as he pulled away. I watched the beam of his flashlight bob around the small space.

"Aha," he said. More scuffling and then a soft yellow glow flooded the space, bringing immediate relief and a cozy ambience.

"Oh, thank God," I muttered.

He handed the flashlight back to me and I swung the beam back over the floor.

"Is that a mattress?"

I shone my flashlight on the stained and dusty old mattress spanning half the floor.

"Only the best for you, Oliver. There's a ratty old loveseat too."

"Holy shit. That looks like it's about a hundred years old. The mattress too."

"I brought some clean blankets from the bunkhouse."

"Yay?"

He laughed. "Oh, come on. We're at a fucking ranch, Oliver, not the Four Seasons. Suck it up."

I raised my eyebrows. "Oh. You're going to say that to me, are you? Clean mattress or dirty, I fully plan to...*suck... it...up.*"

I gazed about me, trying not to worry too much about creepy-crawlies and focus on what we'd come here for. The beam of the flashlight landed on a bit of rope coiled in the corner.

"Hmm," I said.

"What?"

"There's some rope here," I said.

"Probably full of spiders," Puck commented.

"Oh fuck. You're right. Goddammit."

Puck lifted his backpack with a grin. "Good thing I brought some, then."

I blinked. "You brought rope? You brought *your own* bondage rope?"

"No, Oliver. I just brought rope. Why is it automatically going to be used on me?"

I closed my eyes, the desire inside me brimming over.

"Because," I said, lips suddenly dry. "Because it's all I've been dreaming about. But if you're not into it..."

"Oliver, I *brought* the fucking rope."

Had he packed it in his suitcase? Had he anticipated he might have the opportunity for some bondage fun outside of the stables? Or had he gotten it from Kamal? Something told me I didn't want to know.

Once we had covered the stained surface of the mattress with the soft blankets, the shed felt more civilized and more conducive to a night of unbridled lust. Puck tossed a bundle of black bondage rope onto the mattress. "There you go. Whatever will you do with that, Oliver?"

I let a smile steal over my features. I loved playful Puck. I leaned down and picked up the rope, smoothing it between my fingers and thumbs and regarding Puck contemplatively.

"I won't be able to decide until you're naked."

He grinned and started to take off his clothes while I watched with avid interest.

"Is this your rope, Puck?"

"Whose else would it be?"

"You brought this all the way here, when you knew the ranch would have everything needed to keep you in your place as a ponyboy?"

He blushed. "I really like bondage, okay? I thought I might have the opportunity to tie someone up, or...*get* tied up. I knew I wasn't gonna be a ponyboy *all* the time."

By now he had his T-shirt off and was pushing down his jeans and boxer briefs. His half-hard cock bobbed in front of him as mine pushed against the fly of my pants.

"What do you want to be? Right now?" I said, about to combust with desire.

"Huh?"

I let my words hang in the air while Puck's cock fattened up right in front of me.

He didn't look at me, only concentrated on folding his clothes and placing them in a neat pile while my hands itched to touch him.

"Would you be my ponyboy?"

His head jerked up, and he gazed at me from beneath a bit of hair that had flopped forward. He touched the tip of his tongue to the metal ring in his lip and arched a brow.

"There's not much room to trot in here."

I smiled, my breaths coming quick.

"I don't need you to trot," I said.

Puck crossed his arms in front of his chest. His dick was pointing at me. His pants were around his ankles. Slowly, deliberately, he turned away and bent to the laces of his docs.

I almost choked on my fucking tongue. Because, suddenly, Puck's bare ass was lit by the soft light from the lamp as he leisurely undid his boots and removed them.

Time seemed to stand still. I watched the muscles in his thighs twitch and followed the curve of his ass with my gaze as he pulled his pants off and tossed them aside. I guess he was too preoccupied to fold them.

He said, "I'm leaving my socks on because the floor is filthy."

"Come here. Sit down," I said, because I had an idea.

Puck straightened and moved to sit on the mattress.

He eyed me warily as I dropped the bundle of rope beside him and went to gather up his bubble-gum boots where he'd left them.

Puck scooted backwards, his body lean and lithe and gorgeous, watching me with unabashed curiosity as I knelt and held up one boot.

"What are you doing, Oliver?"

"I'm putting these boots back on you. Because they are so pretty—" I swallowed thickly. "—and I want you to wear them, while I do nasty, nasty things to you."

Our gazes met and held, and I swear it was a good thing

there wasn't anything actually combustible in here because the energy between us could have set off an explosion.

"Fuck," he breathed, leaning back on his elbows and lifting his sock-covered foot.

I carefully slid his boot on, tugging firmly as his heel found its place, while Puck deliberately let his knee fall to the side as I tied the rainbow laces, giving me a glimpse of the dark cleft between his cheeks. As I lifted my gaze to see, he leisurely wrapped a hand around his cock and stroked it, watching me.

"You're good with knots," he said as I tied the laces of his boot into a double bow.

"Yes." I glanced up and smiled. "I did some sailing in my youth."

This made Puck snort a laugh. "You sound like you're fifty. You're still *in* your youth."

"I'll be thirty-one in a few months. I'm not as young as you."

"Good. I *like* older men," Puck said, lifting his other foot so I could slide the remaining boot onto it. While I tugged the heel, he slid two fingers over his balls and pressed them against his taint, closing his eyes with pleasure.

"Oh my fucking God," I whispered. "You are the worst.

How am I supposed to concentrate on what I'm doing?"

"Correction, I am the *best*," Puck said. He slipped the index finger of his other hand in his mouth, sucked on it, then, lifting his ass slightly off the mattress, he reached down and worked it into his hole, making a high breathy sound that went straight down my cock and into my balls.

I dropped his booted foot, and lunged forward, covering his body with mine and latching onto his mouth with a furious need. The intensity of my sudden onslaught forced Puck onto his back. He brought both hands up to cup my face as we breathed into each other, tasting and teasing and reveling in our mingled scents.

Puck groaned and thrust up against me. "Jesus, Oliver. You're about to bust through your jeans."

"I know, I know," I said, swiping my tongue against his and shivering at the sensation of it. "Can't help it. You are so fucking hot."

"Did you want me when you saw me that first time? In the paddock?"

"Oh God. Yes. That fucking tail."

"I know," he moaned, "That was so goddamn hot. Humiliating and hot and, fuck, I wanted you so much after that."

I groaned and deepened the kiss, as Puck reached

between us and popped the button of my jeans, tugging the zipper down. In a moment he had my cock in his hot hand.

"Oh," I panted. "Fuck."

"Girthy." Puck hissed, squeezing me. "But I knew that already. I've been dreaming about this cock."

"Really?"

"Yeah. Want you to fuck me. But first I want you to tie me up. And finish lacing my boot, if you please. I want to be dignified in my debasement."

I laughed, kissing his chin and neck and chest as I withdrew down his body to properly tie that pink boot. My fingers trembled as I knotted the laces. Then I knelt on the ratty mattress. I picked up the bundle of rope and loosened it, letting it fall to Puck's naked belly in soft loops.

"Make me your ponyboy," he said, gazing up at me with lust-blown pupils. "I want you to ride the fuck out of me."

Oh dear God.

"Fuck, yes. I want to do that."

Puck sat up and placed his fists together.

"Good ponyboy," I said, looping the black rope over his wrist.

He smiled. "I'll be good for you, Oliver. I'll be so good."

"I know you will."

I fastened his wrists securely enough that he couldn't break free, but not so tight it would restrict his blood flow.

"Now what?" Puck said when that was done.

I grabbed the taut rope between his wrists and pulled him to a sitting position. "Bend your knees and put your boots together."

"Okay," he smiled.

I winked. "Okay, *what?*"

His pupils dilated further in the dim lamplight. There was barely any colour around them now.

"Okay, *sir.*"

I thrilled to that title from his lips, and tried not to pay attention to his soft, fast breaths and the humming energy of his body as I quickly roped his ankles together. Once I'd secured them, I fastened his bound wrists to the rope between his ankles, so that he sat in a hunched position, unable to move, his pink boots the only item of clothing on him.

"How does that feel?"

He tested his restraints and grunted.

"Confining." He flashed his eyes to mine. "Debasing. *Humiliating.*"

I raised my eyebrows. "And we like that?"

He nodded, licking his lips. "Oh yeah."

I smiled but didn't say anything as I pushed his shoulder so that he tipped over and lay on his side, completely vulnerable to my whims.

"Fuck," he said.

"You need a safeword."

"No, I don't. I'm game for whatever."

"Puck. Give me a word."

He laughed. "I don't know. Uh, 'skinny dip.'"

"Okay. Promise to say it if things get too intense, or too...anything?"

"I promise. Oliver?"

"What?"

"I'm dying. I'm burning up. *Do something.*"

"All right." I quickly divested myself of clothing, tossing each piece so that it landed where Puck could see.

"You bastard." He craned his neck, but I was behind him, deliberately hiding from view. "I want to see you."

"Not much to see, Puck. My cock is fucking hard though. Wow, I've never seen it so big. It's leaking for you."

Puck whimpered, his body shuddering, as I knelt and snugged up behind him where he lay. When my hot, hard, *wet* cock hit his lower back he made a desperate sound and cursed.

I had brought a tube of lube with me, and I held it in front of his face. "Hey, can you get the top off for me?"

Puck groaned and struggled, cursing me and whimpering.

I kissed his freckled shoulder and smiled against his warm skin. "Kidding. I guess I can manage it."

"Oliver," Puck whined. "Oliver..."

"What?" I said, putting the lube down and ripping open a condom. I groaned as I unrolled it onto my cock, knowing Puck could hear every bit of what I was doing but couldn't see. I could be sadistic when it suited me.

"Please...please. I'm dying..."

"You're not dying. If you need to be untied, use your safeword."

He made a loud grunt, struggling hard and then lying still. "Just fuck me. Please fuck me."

"I'm going to fuck you, my sweet little pony. Hold your fucking horses."

Puck made a sound that was half laugh, half whimper. My gaze kept sliding over his utterly beautiful, captive, form. The black ropes glistened against his pale skin. I could hardly believe this gorgeous boy wanted *me*.

But he did. He absolutely did.

I glanced at his cock and I swear to God it looked like a

rocket ready for takeoff—perfectly straight and sticking up. The head was purple with congestion and fluid leaked down the side of it, in snail trails of shiny moisture.

"You are so *fucking* hard." I reached around and swiped some of the wetness with my finger, putting it into my mouth and slurping loudly.

"Oliver!"

"Okay, okay," I said. "I'm going to get you ready for me."

"Yes," he hissed, head dropping to the mattress, shoulders relaxing.

I lubed up my condom-covered cock and then pressed my slippery fingers against his hole, sliding them around the wrinkled edge and then slipping one inside.

Puck gasped and stuttered, his body tensing.

"Okay?" I asked, holding still for a second.

Puck made a strangled noise but nodded, panting and shuddering, as I pushed my finger in all the way.

"So tight. Fuck, you're *so* tight."

Puck made a helpless noise. "I loosen up real good, once things get going," he panted.

"Well, they're going," I said, adding a second finger while Puck cried out, his cock surging.

"*Fuck*," he said. "You can be rougher. *Please* be rougher."

I stopped trying to think of sexy things to say and concentrated on slicking up his sweet hole, plunging my fingers in and loosening him up like he wanted.

His response was immediate and amplified. I pulled my fingers out and lined up my cock, unable to wait any longer. This had been a long time coming, and I was just as desperate as he was.

I spread those perfect ass cheeks and pressed the head of my cock against the shiny wrinkled skin there. As I breached the muscle and stroked into the plush heat of him, we gasped. Then Puck gave a long, low groan and cursed as I sank in all the way.

"You okay?" I whispered, dying to move but worried about Puck.

"I'm fine. I'm fine. Just fuck me. Please, Oliver. Fuck me hard. Make me forget about everything but *this*."

"Okay. Okay."

I wrapped my arms around his bound body and started to move, the heat and slick softness a refuge from the external world. I forgot we were in a filthy shack in the middle of the woods. I didn't care. All I knew was that this beautiful, broken man had let me in, had trusted me with his body and his soul and I was going to make this good for him. I'd make him forget everything he was struggling with except for the bonds on his ankles and wrists, and the breaching of his body, and the igniting of his blood.

My own grunts accompanied Puck's soft cries as I found a rhythm and kept to it, my hips snapping hard and short to maintain it, while Puck's body responded in marvellous ways.

"I can't hold off, Puck," I said, not wanting to disappoint him but needing to be clear. "You are so fucking hot. So fucking gorgeous. So fucking sexy."

I slid my hand between his thighs and wrapped my still-slick fingers around his cock, pumping it as I thrust into him. "Come for me. Shoot for me."

With a loud, strangled cry he came over my knuckles as I pounded into him, the hot flush of his release sending me over the edge.

I yelled as I came, biting down on his shoulder, my breaths wild and loud, noises I'd never made before, ripping out of me at the intensity of it all.

The walls of the shed echoed with our cries and then everything fell silent except for our panting breaths and the heartbeat in my ears, that gradually slowed while I clutched Puck to me and peppered his head with kisses.

"Oh my God, Oliver. Jesus."

"You okay? I'm sorry," I said. I hadn't meant to get that out of control.

"For what? That was...that was..." he groaned. "I don't think I'm a virgin anymore."

My heart stopped in my chest for a moment, then chugged forward.

"What? You're not—" I grabbed the base of the condom and pulled out of him, freaking out a little. But the sound of his sudden laughter gave me comfort and reassurance, even as I wanted to spank him for being so provocative.

"It's a joke. A joke. But I feel like you've taken my virginity again. Because it's never been like *that*."

I sighed with relief, moving around so I crouched in front of him, taking his sweet face in my hands. His cheeks were red, and there were beads of sweat on his forehead, dampening his hair.

"I liked that. I liked it a lot."

I held his gaze for several long moments, until a broad, exhausted grin spread over Puck's face.

"So...that was something we did."

"Shit, I need to untie you because, if I don't, I might have to fuck you all over again."

"Normally, I'd be into it. But it's pretty late and—" he

yawned. "I need my beauty sleep."

I fumbled with the ropes and finally got them all off him, only to be bowled over. I found myself on my back on the blankets, staring up at him.

"That was so, so fucking good, Oliver, and just what I needed."

"Same here. You're incredible."

He laughed and bent to kiss me, hard and wet and deep. I threaded my fingers in his hair to keep him there for long, luxurious, moments.

When we pulled apart Puck glanced between his legs. "Goddammit. I can't get enough of you."

"I seem to have the same problem."

"Want to do it again tomorrow night?" he whispered, nuzzling my cheek and nipping at my chin.

"Oh, fuck yes. Every night."

Puck pulled back and smiled. "I hope Adam's paying you well. Because from now on, you'll be working twice as hard."

CHAPTER TWELVE

REPARATIONS

OR

A CHANGE OF ATTITUDE

WE DID MEET the next night. And the next. And then Puck had to take a break because, between the horsetail butt plug and the pounding I was giving him every day, he was getting sore.

"Kamal saw me wince when he put the plug in, and he questioned me about it. I implied it was only his rough treatment making me sore, but I think he knew there was more to it. He didn't make me wear it anyway. Which I was very thankful for."

We had met at the bunkhouse, walked to the lake, and swum out to the dock in the moonlight. The water felt heavenly cool and crisp on my skin after the humidity of the day. We'd goofed around in the water, laughing like eight-year-olds and trying to dunk each other. Finally, we'd climbed onto the platform and now lay on our backs, staring up at the stars.

"When did you first realize you were gay?" Puck asked, reaching down to take my hand and stroke his finger over my skin.

I turned my head to look at him because Puck, naked and wet in the moonlight, was a sight to behold. His pale skin shone in the silver light and the beads of water on his shoulders glistened like promises.

"Oh, I don't know. Seventh grade, I think? You?"

Puck laughed. "In the womb? No, really, I think I always knew. I was drawn to girls as friends, not sexual partners." He shuddered. "Yeah, no."

"Is your family okay with it?"

"Sure. It was like they always knew too. I'm not sure how because I don't think I'm girly. Do *you* think I'm girly?" He met my gaze and raised the eyebrow with the barbell in it.

"Well, I don't think there's anything wrong with femboys. But you don't strike me as being one."

"Hmm. That sounds like a challenge."

My gaze drifted along his slim, sleekly muscled body. "For what it's worth, I think you'd rock a plaid skirt and some thigh-highs."

He laughed. "Fuck. You know I look fabulous in anything I put on."

"Oh, do I ever," I said with a smile, twining our fingers together. "Especially the ropes."

"That was fun. I liked it."

I grinned. "I could tell."

Puck met my gaze. "Did you like it?" he asked, grinning because he knew that fucking answer.

"I loved it. So much."

We gazed at each other until Puck's smile faded and he turned back to the vista of tiny lights above us.

"I think...I think I want to call Elijah."

I waited to see if he had more to say.

He continued. "But I really don't want to call him from the front room or the washroom," he murmured, glancing at me.

"You want to use my room? I'm sure Adam wouldn't mind."

Puck sat up halfway. "Would that be okay?"

"Sure. I'll let you in and then disappear for a bit. No problem."

He blinked quickly then brushed at his face with the back of his hand. "Thank you. I'd appreciate that." He stayed propped on his elbow for a bit, then rolled over and climbed on top of me. He put his hands on either side of my shoulders, supporting himself on the wooden planks.

"How come you're so nice to me?" he said, gazing down, his damp hair falling forward. He shook his head and showered me with water droplets.

His sudden move had surprised me, and I didn't know what to say. I decided to go for humour.

"Because you have a great ass. Looks good with a tail in it."

Puck grinned. "Most of these guys have nice asses."

"I wouldn't know."

He raised his eyebrows.

I slid my hands along his sides and cupped the globes of his absolutely perfect behind.

"I only like this one."

I lifted my hand and gave that ass cheek a firm slap that shoved Puck against me in a wonderful way and caused the muscle to jiggle. It also made his firming dick push against my stomach. His eyes fluttered shut for a second, and when they opened, the pupils had blown wide and dark.

"Oh, Oliver. You've started something now," he said, his gaze floating over my face like he was trying to memorize it.

"Good," I breathed, gazing up at him like he was the brightest star in the sky. His beauty was blinding.

"Fuck," he cursed, then kissed me softly and moaned against my lips.

I encircled him with my arms and nudged his pretty mouth open so I could delve into his warm, wet depths, while my cock filled and strained against his thigh. I groaned and thrust against him.

"Oh," I groaned.

"Nope. You can't fuck me, Oliver. I'm too sore."

"I don't want to fuck you."

He pulled back and lifted an eyebrow. "What? Why not?"

I laughed at his wounded expression.

"Because I love this. I could do this all night."

I pressed against him again, and he shoved his cock

against my hip, grinning.

"Yeah, okay. That's true."

"I don't even want to come. I just want to feel this way forever," I murmured, astonishingly content.

He kissed me again, and we lay together and made out like teenagers until the muggy heat and relentless mosquitos forced us into the water.

Finally, we headed for shore, got mostly dressed, and walked hand in hand back to the bunkhouse, where I kissed Puck good night and returned to my lonely room, floating on the oppressively humid air.

*

I SPOKE TO Adam about letting Puck use my room to call his friend, and Adam said that was fine. So, after Puck's morning ponyboy session the next day, he met me on the porch and went to get his phone.

He checked his emails as soon as we got to my room.

"Oh. Elijah's parents have brought him home. Maybe things are looking better," Puck said. He flipped about on his phone for a few minutes, then asked if he could use my shower, since he'd only gotten a quick hose down in the grooming barn.

"Yeah, of course."

I tried going over some of the images I'd posted to my computer while he was in there, but it was difficult to concentrate knowing that Puck was naked and soapy and *right the fuck there*. But I was an adult and didn't act on my impulses. He probably needed to psyche himself up for this phone call.

After what seemed like eons, he returned to the main part of the room, fully dressed, with damp, tousled hair that made my heart ache. He looked so vulnerable and delicate, his forehead creased with concern.

"Do you think I'm making the right call?" he said. "What if this makes me feel worse? Or, what if it makes Elijah feel worse? What if he's sleeping, and I wake him up?"

"Puck—"

"Maybe I should just wait and see him when I get home."

I was silent for a moment and then put my words together very carefully.

"I think...that Elijah will probably be very glad to hear from you."

Puck nodded, avoiding my gaze. "But what if I say all the wrong things? I'm no good at this stuff, Oliver." He picked up his phone and turned it on. Then put it to sleep and returned it to the table. "Fuck. I don't know."

I stood from my chair, going over and pulling him against me, holding him tight to give him what encouragement I could offer. His arms wrapped around me in an automatic gesture that made me disproportionately happy.

"You'll do fine. He'll be glad to hear your voice."

Puck nodded and took a deep breath. "Right."

I released him and grabbed my keys. "I'll be back in a half hour. Make yourself at home."

I took hold of the doorknob.

"Wait."

"Yeah?"

He stood where I'd left him, in his ripped jeans shorts and the LEGO Star Wars shirt.

"Can—can you stay?"

"Yeah, sure. Of course." I was stunned he'd asked. But I would do anything he wanted.

"Okay," he said, appearing relieved. "I need...moral support. Or something. Or someone to help if I start to panic."

"Sure," I said. "I can do that." I put my keys back on the dresser and sat on the edge of the bed.

Puck nodded. "Okay. All right."

He picked up his phone again, staring at it with trepidation. "Oh, God, why am I so nervous?"

"It'll be all right."

"Jeez, I hope so. But what if he's pissed that I took so long to actually call and talk to him?"

I grinned. "Well, in a way, that would be a sign that he's well enough to get pissed with people. Right?"

Puck shrugged. "Yeah. Maybe. But how will I explain?"

"Hey, it's okay to admit you were scared and full of feelings you didn't understand. It would be better for him to know that his situation affected you strongly than for him to think you don't care."

Puck nodded soberly. "I *do* care. Of course, I fucking care. I *hate* that this happened. If he'd just listened to me when I'd told him—"

"Yeah. He probably realizes now that he should have listened to you."

"Yeah."

"Puck, baby," I said because he seemed like a little kid right now and I wanted to use the endearment. "Can I say that?"

Puck met my gaze and blushed. It was the sweetest thing in the world. *He* was the sweetest thing in the world. "You can say that to me any time," he said, keeping his gaze averted.

Warmth spread inside my chest. "Call him."

He met my gaze and nodded once. He woke his phone and put the call through, then held my gaze as he waited for a response. After several seconds, he raised his eyebrows in a silent question.

"Maybe they can't get to the phone right away," I suggested.

"I don't want to bother—"

His gaze broke from mine as the call was answered. I couldn't hear what was said, but I could hear a voice.

"Oh, hi, Mrs. Alderman. It's Puck... Yeah, I know, I'm sorry it's taken me so long to call... Okay...yes...really?"

Puck seemed to brighten. He glanced at me just for one second, but I could see the relief there.

"That's amazing...yes... I know he is... I'd love to speak to him if you think he'd be up for it?"

There was a pause while Puck shifted his feet and waited.

"Hey Elijah," he said, when a deeper-toned voice came from his phone. "I know, man, I am *so*, so sorry... Yeah... I feel like such a douche." He laughed. "You should...definitely."

His gaze flashed to mine with such affection and relief it warmed my heart.

"Really? Fuck, really? Oh, god..." His face crumpled and

he started to cry. I resisted the urge to go over there, because him crying was a good thing, even though what it meant might be not so good. He nodded and tried to rally, swiping at his face with his free hand as he sat on the bed. "Sorry, I...that's so amazing. I can hardly believe it."

He flashed me a smile and a thumbs up.

"Yeah, I met this guy, actually. Yeah...oh, he's *so* hot. You have no idea. And you wouldn't believe where I am right now... Nope...I'll tell you when I see you in person...I'm here for another month... I know...but I needed to get away." Puck laughed again, and it was such a wonderful sound. "I'll call you again in a few days, okay? I'm so glad to hear things are going well, man. Stay strong, okay? I love you... I'm sorry I didn't call you sooner... Okay...bye."

Puck ended his call and blinked back more emotion, his breaths shaky. "I could really use a hug right now, Oliver."

I jumped up from my spot on the bed and wrapped him in my arms.

Puck snugged his forehead into the crook of my neck, holding onto me. He spoke then, his voice muffled against my shirt.

"He's got feeling in his legs now. He's going to be able to walk. It's going to take time and lots of rehab, but he's going to be okay."

I hugged Puck tighter and pressed my lips to his cheek. "I'm so glad you called him."

"Yeah, me too. He basically told me I was a dick and a chicken. But you know what? It felt good to hear him cuss me out. Like you said, he sounded like his old self, y'know?"

"Sure."

Puck pulled away and seemed to collect himself.

"Is it okay if I use your room to call him again in a few days? I guess I could just call him from downstairs, since everything seems okay, but—"

"Of course, you can. Any time."

Puck shoved his hands in his pockets and gazed at me with gratitude. "Thanks, Oliver."

"Do you want to sleep here tonight?"

"Uh, am I allowed to?"

"Oh, so now you're all about the rules?"

"I really don't want to get kicked off this ranch, Oliver."

I held his hands and played with his fingers. "I'll ask Adam. If he says no, then maybe I can sneak into the bunkhouse or something."

"You're dedicated."

"Yes. I am."

Adam gave the okay, and Puck came back to my room that night after supper.

We didn't even do anything other than snuggle and talk about everything under the sun, until we fell asleep. In the morning, Puck woke me to say he was heading to the grooming barn.

*

THE NEXT TIME Puck came up to my room, we did more than just chat.

"Hmm," he said. "I suppose I should thank you somehow."

I laughed. "For what?"

He shrugged. "For helping to dig my head out of my ass."

"You don't have to thank me."

We gazed at each other. Then Puck took his hands from his pockets and moved toward me, fingers going to my shirt. He untucked it from my pants.

"Maybe I want to thank you..."

I rested my hands on his narrow hips. "Well, if you really want to thank me."

Puck grinned from ear-to-ear. "I *really* want to thank you." He glanced at the door. "Did you lock it?"

"Yeah."

"Good. Do you think Adam will care that I'm up here... *thanking* you?"

I took Puck's chin in my hand and planted an eager kiss on his lips. "I think Adam will probably mind his own business. If we're circumspect."

"What the fuck does that mean, Oliver?"

I laughed. "It means if you can keep from screaming my name when I make you come."

Puck winked. "No promises."

He did fairly well, but I ended up stuffing a pair of clean underwear into his mouth to keep him quiet, which he seemed to enjoy. This was after he'd given me a soul-destroying blow job and I'd had to bite my own tongue to keep quiet. Now I was licking him all over his balls and ass and driving him completely crazy, especially because he couldn't give way to unhindered vocalizations.

His muffled groans made me hard all over again. He was completely malleable today, after the good news he'd had the day before, with regards to his friend. He was open and vulnerable and able to relax for the first time in what was probably ages. And I took advantage of that, breaking him apart until he panted my name against the wad of fabric in his mouth.

"Okay, fine. Do you want to come?"

"Uh, uh!" he groaned, voice harsh and desperate, words strangled by the impromptu gag.

"Stick out your ass for me, ponyboy." I said, shoving his knees forward so his rear went up, and I had plenty of access to his cock.

"Gug," he mumbled indistinctly, spreading his legs and grasping the bedcover in his fists.

"Good boy. Such a good boy. Such a delicious pony."

I lapped at his hole again, then lubed up my fingers and got to work, pumping him and stretching him. I wasn't going to fuck him, but I wanted to get him off like fireworks on Canada Day.

I felt cocky and in control. I liked it.

"Say, 'I'm such a good boy, Oliver.'"

"Ung-gugged," Puck moaned.

"Try to say it."

"Ugh?"

"Because I love to hear you struggle."

"U-a-hug-gah."

I interpreted that as *You're a sick man*, which was accurate. I laughed.

"Yep. Now *say* it." I had two fingers in Puck's ass and I'd located the spot I wanted to tease and stroke until he shouted my name and came all over my bedsheets.

"Ang-hug-uh"—he cried out as my hand circled his cock—"gug-guh!"

"Oliver," I prompted, pumping his cock with one hand and fucking him gently with my fingers.

"UH-UH-UHGUGA!" he shouted through the gag, spurting hard and shaking under my hand.

I truly hoped none of the trainers were on the floor at this time. They should have been either getting some lunch or preparing for their afternoon sessions.

Puck rode the pleasure of his orgasm and collapsed to the bedding, right into his own wet spot.

He grunted with exhaustion. I took the gag out and kissed him.

"You bastard," he murmured.

I kissed him again. "Sweet baby."

He sighed and closed his eyes, a smile on his sweaty face.

*

WE DIDN'T MEET the next day because I had work to do. Real work, involving polishing the images I'd chosen and putting a slideshow together for the weekend. I had let him know I'd be busy all day, and he'd said he didn't mind, and he had a good book to read in the bunkhouse. And that maybe he should show a bit more interest in the other ponyboys. I'd raised my eyes, and he'd stressed that it would be a purely platonic interest, as his ass only had the strength for one sexual attachment at a time, apparently.

The following morning, I wandered over to the arena when I knew Kamal would be training my beautiful boy. Or attempting to train him. I brought my handheld, since I already had enough from the tripod to keep my busy.

The day was stunning—bright and hot—but the hanging humidity had dissipated. Still, sweat beaded on the back of my neck as I approached the second paddock.

Puck was in his basic ponyboy gear, but his arms had been left unbuckled. Probably because there were a couple of low oxers in the paddock this afternoon, and Kamal was having Puck jump over them—a task that would prove extra hard with one's arms pinioned.

Kamal saw me before Puck did. He waved me over and came to meet me at the fence. It was difficult to drag my gaze away from the sweaty young man in leather harness and dirty boots, muscles moving beneath soft skin, as he maneuvered over the small jumps.

"Oliver."

"Kamal."

Kamal folded his arms on the top rail of the fence and assessed me silently for a moment.

"What?"

"Hmm. I don't know what you did, but our ornery little mess of a ponyboy is performing exquisitely today. He's done everything I've asked, without issue."

"What *I* did? I don't know what you're—"

"Although I sincerely doubt a good fucking is what brought on this behaviour." Kamal checked me out in a slow sexual way and smirked. "Although, you never know."

"Oh, please. I'm good, but I'm not that good." I laughed.

Kamal grinned lazily.

We watched Puck, who continued his task, although he had noticed me. He almost lifted a hand to wave but thought better of it and kept his gaze forward, concentrating on what he was doing.

I ran my fingers through my hair. "Anyway, I didn't do anything."

Puck had been the one to initiate his phone call. And I wouldn't be surprised if his agreeable behaviour was due to the weight of his guilt and the precariousness of Elijah's predicament being lifted.

Kamal nodded. "Adam said Puck made a phone call from your room."

"He needed some privacy."

"A personal call?"

I shrugged. I wasn't giving Kamal any other info. He'd have to ask Puck if he wanted details.

"Uh-huh. So, do you think that had anything to do with his change of manner?"

"Probably."

"Well. That's good. I won't ask you any more questions."

"Thanks."

"Okay, Puck," Kamal called out. "You can come over here and take a break."

Puck had just gone over one of the low jumps. He jogged over to us, breathing heavily and rosy with exertion. And... *smiling?*

Kamal ruffled Puck's dark hair. "I'm glad you're feeling more congenial."

"Yeah. Might not last."

"I don't want you to lose that fighting edge completely. I'd like an excuse to punish you once in a while."

"Fuck, I knew it. You're hoping for mistakes, aren't you?"

"Maybe." Kamal grinned. "You're a most beautiful mistake if I ever saw one."

"Don't try to butter me up, now," Puck said, coughing and blushing. He scuffed his boot in the dirt. "You're a cruel, cruel master, Kamal."

"Mmm. And you love every minute of it."

Puck glared at Kamal, a bit of his former attitude resurfacing. "What *now*, sir? Or am I done?"

Kamal gazed back and forth between the two of us, then threw his hands in the air. "Take him to the grooming barn, Oliver. He's done well today and deserves some time off. Maybe you can go for a swim or something."

Chapter Thirteen

PRELUDE TO A PICTURE SHOW

OR

How to Get Soundly Wrecked by the Sweet Boy You Secretly Love

FIVE WEEKS PASSED in a haze of delicious photography and that intoxicating feeling of getting to know someone you admired and lusted for. The other shoe never dropped, and Puck and I found ourselves more and more enamoured of each other. He seemed to settle in once he'd talked to Elijah and learned his friend's future looked much more optimistic.

Who would have thought I'd find someone so suited to me and my brand of loving on a pony play ranch? I guess I was kinkier, and more of a fucking top than I'd thought. This ranch, and this ponyboy, was bringing it out in me.

I waited for Puck outside the grooming barn. When he came out the door he practically jumped into my arms. I grabbed him and fell against the wall so I didn't go over. He wasn't all that heavy, but he moved with the oblivious energy of an excited Labrador retriever.

"A free afternoon at the lake! With the sexy ranch photographer!" Puck said, caging me with his legs and shoving his pelvis against me.

"Oh, my. What have you got there?" I asked.

He winked. "What I always have there. Something to put in your mouth, Mr. Lambert. Or anywhere else you'd like."

I playfully shoved at him. "Aren't we going to the lake?"

"Sure. It's great weather for a swim. And anything else we decide on."

Puck stepped back and took my hand, pulling me off the wall and leading me along the path. When we reached the bunkhouse, Puck ducked inside to grab towels and suntan lotion. When he came out, I was standing with my hands in my pockets, enjoying the summer afternoon.

Puck appeared subdued.

"What's wrong?"

He frowned. "Nobody's there. I bet they're all at the fucking lake. So much for a sexy rendezvous."

"We could...uh...skip the lake and go to the shack." I pretended to brush a piece of lint off his T-shirt. I really only wanted to touch him. "Nobody's going to wonder where we are. We'll just have to be careful coming back."

Puck's smile returned. "Okay. I'll put this stuff back and get a blanket."

"Do you have condoms?"

Puck stared at me, the corner of his lip twitching. He hesitated, glancing at my groin, then meeting my gaze. "Do we need condoms?"

Oh, fuck. The thought of having Puck with no barrier in the way made me lose my mind.

"What?"

"I actually haven't gone bareback with anyone," he admitted. "And it's been a long time since the last guy. But if you're nervous about it–"

I shook my head, smiling at the ground.

"No. I'm not." I met his gaze again. "I was tested for everything last year, and haven't been with anyone since." I ran my fingers through my hair. It was embarrassing to admit although Puck had basically said the same thing.

But I grinned. "You're the one who should be worried."

Puck cocked his head. "Why?"

I scuffed the toe of my shoe in the dirt.

"Because I have plans, ponyboy."

*

IT WAS DIFFERENT making our way to the shack in the day-time—less nerve-racking, what with the pleasant sounds of day birds and the scurry of squirrels all around us, rather than the haunting hoots of owls and the spooky sounds of animals I couldn't identify.

Puck knew the way, and it didn't take long to get there. This time, I was prepared for the decrepit state of the place although it looked a lot dirtier in the sunlight.

As soon as we stepped inside and Puck pulled the door shut, I grabbed him and shoved him against the wall.

"Whoa. Oliver, what the f—"

He didn't have time to say more before I attacked his mouth. The vibrations of his startled laughter reverberated against me as he opened and melted beneath my frenzied assault, letting me take what I wanted. His hands clutched the shirt at my waist, pelvis thrusting against me as we tangled ourselves in a firestorm of lust.

I moaned. "Goddamn."

I couldn't get enough. It was making me desperate and greedy, but my boy was keeping up. He popped the button on my jeans and slipped his hand inside, finding my dick and pulling it up so it could stand unheeded. I winced at first, then groaned as he handled it as roughly as I was handling him.

"Oh, you are so hard for me, old man. *Shit.*" Puck breathed.

I grinned at the insult, tilting his face up so I could attack the arch of his neck with my lips and teeth. I wanted him so bad. I wanted everything.

"How's your ass? Is it sore?" I panted.

"Nope," he said, voice dirty and dark. "I need you inside me."

"Okay. Okay," I said. I glanced at the mattress, which still needed to be covered.

He laughed. "Slow down, old man. You're gonna give yourself a coronary."

I pulled away from him and narrowed my eyes.

"Very funny." I pierced him with my gaze and placed a chaste kiss against his swollen mouth. "Go get the mattress ready so I can fuck you into it."

I swear, his pupils darkened in front of me.

"Fuck," he swore, but he moved away from the wall. I couldn't resist giving his cute-as-hell ass a quick swat.

"Ow. I'm going," he said, as he did my bidding. "Calm your tits, Oliver. We've got all afternoon."

I watched him, loving the sinewy way his body moved as he covered the mattress with the clean black sheet he'd brought.

"There," he said. "Anything else?" He stood beside the covered mattress, gazing at me with what could have been devotion.

"Yeah. Strip. Everything off."

"This is a side of you I really haven't seen before," Puck said, peeling off his shirt. "Glimpses maybe, but never the full dominant vibe. I like it."

I grinned. "Good."

"I need a safeword."

"Yes. You do. Let's use 'beach.'"

"All right. But I don't plan on using it."

"Good," I grinned. "Now lie down on your front with

your arms and legs spread."

He did as I'd asked, body softly golden against the black sheet. He swivelled his head to look at me. "I didn't bring any rope."

"I know. We don't need it. I know you're going to listen to me and do as you're fucking told."

Puck closed his eyes and shuddered. "Yes, Sir."

"That's good. I like that," I said, kneeling on the mattress and sliding my hands to his ass. My thumbs slipped into his crack and I spread those soft, curved cheeks apart. I blew on his pink hole, making him shiver as it winked at me.

"Damn," I hissed. "I should have asked Liv if I could borrow your ponytail."

"Fuck, Oliver. Next time."

I glanced around the shack. "Shit, we should have brought lube."

"I did. It's in my pocket." Puck pointed at the pants he'd thrown aside. I found the small tube in a moment as Puck reached for his cock.

"Don't touch yourself," I said while I greased up his ass to his pleasure-filled sounds. Then I had a thought. If we did it in this position, I'd have to do all the hard work. If I lay on my back, I could make Puck do the heavy lifting.

"Wait a second," I said, flopping down onto the bed beside him. I gazed up at his face, so handsome and young, his expression excited and unguarded.

"What are you doing?"

"I'm relaxing," I said as I pushed down my pants and used the rest of the lube to grease up my cock. "Because you're going to ride *me*, ponyboy."

His eyebrows arched and his gaze went to my erection. He licked his lips. "Oh yeah?"

I nodded. "Yeah."

Puck pushed himself onto his haunches, giving me a skeptical look. "Do you think you're ready for that, Oliver?"

I laughed at the confident tone in his voice. "I think I can handle it."

"Really." Puck's gaze drifted over my body in a way that made all my nerve endings sit up and take notice.

Somehow, the dynamic had changed. I tried to maintain control.

"Get on my cock, Puck. Now."

He shrugged, affecting nonchalance. "Fine. Have it your way."

With the grace of a cat, he stretched himself out and climbed on top of me, causing me to tip my head back to maintain eye contact. He had the most intense look on his face as he stared down at me like a crouched jungle cat transfixing its prey.

"What?" I said.

"Mmm, nothing. Just taking a screen shot in my brain of how you look before you get wrecked."

I grinned at his cheekiness and slapped him across the ass. "Get busy. I want that ass of yours to swallow my cock and do a fucking dance on it."

Puck laughed, the reflex sending a puff of warm cinnamon-scented breath onto my face.

I closed my eyes and inhaled. "I love the smell of that weird toothpaste."

"Me too. I like spicy things in my mouth."

"No kidding."

Puck drew up and positioned himself over me as I grabbed my dick at the base and held it steady. Watching him spread his own cheeks, bumping his hole at the top of my eager cock, almost made me come.

"Oh, fuck," I whimpered. Maybe I should have just done it the other way. I'd be inside him by now, and it would be—" A breath hissed through my teeth as my bare cock suddenly became engulfed in Puck's slippery heat. "Oh, *God.*"

Puck didn't give me time to recover before he pushed down onto the rest of me. I don't know how he took me inside him so easily, but my eyes rolled back in my head as his body gripped my cock in its warmth.

"Oh my God," I moaned, letting go of myself and gripping Puck's knees, to do what, I wasn't sure. Slow him down? Make him go faster? I was out of my depth.

The rawness of having no barrier between us made me giddy and so turned on.

"That's it, Ollie boy. Hold onto something 'cause things are about to get wild."

The confidence in his tone undid me. I'd only gained control in past encounters because he'd let me. Now he had me where he wanted me.

"Hmm? What's that, Ollie?" he said, the casual nickname giving me chills as Puck wiggled himself on my erection, making me stutter and groan. "I can't quite make that out. Oh? You say go easy on you because you're an innocent photographer who's gotten in over his head? Well, not a chance." Puck sighed as he moved on my cock with the skills of a pole dancer. "I'm gonna fuck you till you scream my name and give me your babies."

Holy mother of God.

I gazed up at this banshee that was going to take everything it wanted from me without a qualm and thanked God I'd made the decision to accept Adam's offer to come to the Braided Crop Ranch. Not for the career advancement or the voyeuristic opportunity to catalogue the outrageous amounts of kink that went on here, but because *this* moment of debauchery by the man who had already stolen my heart was something I had needed for a long time.

My mouth opened on a groan as Puck placed his hands over mine and arched his back, lifting up in a serpentine twist and sliding back down, making my cock think it had died and gone to heaven.

It had. Puck's body was a holy shrine. I lay there with wide eyes and parted lips, praying silently to the sweaty priest above me.

"Oh, fuck yeah," he growled. "Your cock feels like a torpedo. It's fucking perfect." He rocked on my dick, causing ripples of sensation to shoot up through my whole body.

"Puck, Puck," I panted, gripping his knees, trying to ground myself when this was getting out of control too fast. "Oh, my fucking God. Puck!"

"What? You gonna come?" He laughed, maintaining his rhythm as his dick bounced in the air, shiny with his arousal.

"I—I—" I stuttered, as the pleasure increased and there was nothing I could do to stop it. Puck's skilled writhing pulled it out of me as easily as a man uncorking a bottle, and with another breath I exploded, my body stiffening as lightning shot from my balls and rolled out my cock. "Aw, fuck. Fuck! Oh, fuck."

I made the most embarrassing noise as I came, gazing wide-eyed at the glory that was Puck doing aerobics on my cock and smiling like he'd known all along I was his bitch but had waited until this moment to show me.

He sat down hard and jerked his cock so viciously I worried he'd take off into the air. Instead, his breath hitched, and he came, cock shooting all over me as I throbbed inside of him, his throat issuing a long, intense groan as he gave himself up to it.

For long moments, we lay there blinking at each other, letting the intensity subside and the real world break in.

"What...*the fuck*...was that?" I whispered. "Am I alive?"

"Seems like it. That was the *Puck wants to fuck you into the ground* special. You like?"

I sighed, still scrambling to rearrange my brain cells. "I don't think *like* is the...right word."

"Well, you survived it. That's something." He smirked,

flicking some jizz onto my chest with his finger. "I did a Pollock on you. Sorry."

I glanced down at where Puck's spunk had splattered onto the skin of my abdomen, then met his gaze. "No, I like it. I love it even."

He grinned. "You dirty, dirty man. And here I thought you were after me for my brain."

I cocked an eyebrow. "On a pony-play ranch?"

Puck laughed. "Okay. Well, sure. But you have to admit, I'm smarter than most of these dudes."

"Well, you're more of a smart-*ass*, that's for sure."

Puck slid off my dick and propped himself on his elbow. "I don't think you should be maligning my ass after it just sent you spiralling through the Milky Way." He swirled a bit of cooling jizz with his fingertip.

"Fine. I take it back."

"Oh, you'll take it front *and* back if I want you to." Puck realized how ridiculous he was starting to sound and cackled a laugh. "Sorry. I'm a bit punchy right now. That was...epic."

"Yes, it was."

He twined his hand with mine as we gazed at the roof of the shed.

"We should really attack this place with a couple of

brooms if we want to keep coming here," Puck said.

"There are a lot of cobwebs up there. Probably tons of spiders." I sighed. "What if one drops onto me?" I started to get up, but Puck held onto my hand tightly to prevent me.

"Then I will vanquish it in a blaze of fury." He rolled onto his side and placed a gentle kiss on my lips. "I'll protect you, Oliver. Always."

*

ON FRIDAY, ADAM and Kamal set up a projector that I could connect to my laptop in order to show everyone a selection of the best images. Since the weather forecast was clear the communal supper was postponed until eight, so we could watch the slideshow of the photos when the sun started to go down around nine o'clock.

I was excited. I was pleased with the photos, and I hoped they impressed everyone, particularly Adam, Kamal, and one ponyboy in particular. The ponyboy who kept shooting me shy glances and winks when nobody else was looking.

Puck had hung out with Lincoln and Alex during the meal, keeping his distance from me. I didn't mind. I knew that even though we weren't fooling Adam or Kamal, and likely the other ponyboys realized there was something going on, Puck got a kick out of the fact that we were fucking behind everybody's backs. I kind of liked that, too, although it was starting to feel a bit ridiculous to deny what was so obvious. But if it made Puck happy, I'd keep up the ruse.

Once darkness fell and the meal had been cleared away, I connected my laptop to the projector, and Kamal clapped his hands together.

"All right, all right. Settle down, you hooligans. It's time for a presentation."

"Yes, SIR!" Someone called out. I was surprised it wasn't Puck.

There was general laughter. But everyone did settle down, and Adam took over from Kamal.

"As you know, Oliver has been at our kinky ranch on an important assignment. And that assignment is to capture what he can of our day-to-day activities, in as artistic a way as possible, so we can post these photos to our website and social feeds in order to let people know what to expect and what the Braided Crop Ranch is all about."

Everyone applauded and a couple of people whistled.

"Tonight, we have a selection of the most...delicious... images that I think I've ever seen. Oliver has taken this assignment and run with it, producing a plethora of incredible photos starring"—he gestured at the crowd of ponyboys and trainers—"all of you."

Again, applause and laughter filled the night air.

"But nobody will know it's you as we have been extremely careful not to reveal any identifying features in these photos. This also leads to a wonderful sense of universality and timelessness in the images, which adds to their appeal. But enough talk. Let's get started."

Adam nodded to me and I projected the first image onto the wall of the main house.

Gasps sounded, along with muttered curses.

I'd chosen this particular photo because it captured the sense of restraint and submission required in the arena, when a ponyboy was ready for his training session and waiting to be taken in hand.

The ponyboy in the photo was Lincoln, but that didn't signify at all. The shot of his arms pinioned by the leather armbands, the back of his head as it bowed, with the metal buckle of the ball gag light against his dark hair, and a glimpse of the scuffed toes of his Docs over his shoulder, gave the viewer the impression of a supplicant awaiting orders. It was an affecting shot with the background out of focus and the black leather accoutrements of the regular tack sharply defined.

I took a breath and clicked through to the next one.

It was a close-up of a cock in the steel cage. I was the only person who knew it belonged to Puck. The photo was incredible, with the shine of the steel echoed in the sparkles of pre-ejaculate that dripped from the bulging red tip. A glistening pearl of fluid was stretched toward the bottom of the shot but remained connected to the glans by a spider's silky thread.

Someone groaned. Someone else said, "That is so fucking hot."

I clicked through to the next shot, which was the image of Kamal's hand in mid-act of pumping a ponyboy's cock in reward. Everyone here could tell it was Kamal's forearm and hand by the dark hair that grew in delicate whorls there, but people who weren't frequent clients of the BCR wouldn't know.

I heard Kamal's soft laughter and his muttered, "Jesus," as the ponyboys cursed again.

"I'm gonna need Kamal's assistance after this slideshow," Joshua said.

Kamal turned. "I don't give out freebies. You have to work for that."

I risked a glance at Puck. He seemed riveted to the

photo, his back straight and hands curled at his sides. But he side-eyed me and quirked his lip in acknowledgement, nodding briefly.

Image after image clicked by, detailing the life of the ponyboys at the Braided Crop Ranch in vivid colour—in the grooming barn and arena and out in the fresh air of the paddock.

I'd included the shot of Puck pissing into the grass that I'd taken that first morning, and when it went up I heard him gasp. The photo had been taken from the side and only the folded material of his jeans could be seen, outlined by the golden rays from the early morning sun. An ethereal cloud of vapour collected in front of him, looking like something out of a fairy story and not the result of Puck's warm piss hitting the cold grass.

"Jesus, Oliver," he said. I glanced over, worried I'd upset him by sharing this private moment.

But his gaze met mine with awe and subdued appreciation. He stood and walked to me. My finger froze on the laptop key as Puck gracefully lowered himself into my lap, surrounded me with his arms, and nuzzled into my neck.

A comforting warmth spread from Puck's languid body sharing its heat with me, and also from his public show of affection and the soft clapping of the watching crowd.

Laughter and muttered sentiments such as, "Finally" and "I told you so" wrapped us with acceptance and kindness.

I took my hand off the keyboard and folded my arms around him, kissing his cheek and whispering words of gratitude into his ear for claiming me in front of everyone. I didn't know what the future held for us beyond our time at the Braided Crop Ranch. But I was determined to find out if this powerful thing between us was as significant as it felt.

Because I knew by that point in my life that a connection this strong, this intense, and this unrelenting was something to hold onto with both hands and a whole, fiercely beating heart.

ABOUT AE LISTER

AE Lister is a Canadian non-binary author with a vivid imagination and a head full of unique and interesting characters. They write explicit, adult LGBTQ+ romance. They also write much less graphic Young Adult LGBTQ+ romance under Alison Lister.

Email

alison@aelister.com

Facebook

www.facebook.com/aelisterauthor

Facebook

www.facebook.com/groups/listersloop

Instagram AE Lister

/www.instagram.com/aelisterauthor

Instagram Alison Lister

www.instagram.com/alisonlisterya

Website AE Lister

www.aelister.com

Website Alison Lister

www.alisonlister.ca

Bookbub

www.bookbub.com/authors/ae-lister

Newsletter Sign-up

www.landing.mailerlite.com/webforms/landing/q5g0u0

Other NineStar books by this author

The Braided Crop Ranch Series

Stable Hand

Ponyboy

Dark Horse

CONNECT WITH NINESTAR PRESS

WWW.NINESTARPRESS.COM

WWW.FACEBOOK.COM/NINESTARPRESS

WWW.FACEBOOK.COM/GROUPS/NINESTARNICHE

WWW.TWITTER.COM/NINESTARPRESS

WWW.INSTAGRAM.COM/NINESTARPRESS

www.ingramcontent.com/pod-product-compliance
Lightning Source LLC
Chambersburg PA
CBHW060251100726
47907CB00003B/841